The Brides of Midsummer

The Brides of Midsummer

VILHELM MOBERG

Translated from the Swedish by
GUDRUN BRUNOT

 Minnesota Historical
Society Press

The publication of this book was supported with funding from the
Dale S. and Elizabeth D. Hanson Fund for Swedish American History.

Originally published as *Brudarnas Källa, Legend om de bofasta*,
©1974 by Albert Bonniers Forlag, Stockholm. Translation
©2013 by Gudrun Brunot. New material ©2014 by the
Minnesota Historical Society.

For information, write to the Minnesota Historical Society Press,
345 Kellogg Blvd. W., St. Paul, MN 55102-1906.

www.mhspress.org

The Minnesota Historical Society Press is a member of the
Association of American University Presses.
Manufactured in the United States of America
10 9 8 7 6 5 4 3 2 1

International Standard Book Number
ISBN: 978–0–87351–920–5 (paper)
ISBN: 978–0–87351–935–9 (e-book)

Library of Congress Cataloging-in-Publication Data

Moberg, Vilhelm, 1898–1973.
[Brudarnas källa. English]
The brides of midsummer / Vilhelm Moberg ; Translated from
the Swedish by Gudrun Brunot.
pages cm.
"Originally published as Brudarnas Kalla,
Legend om de bofasta, 1974 by Albert Bonniers."
ISBN 978-0-87351-920-5 (pbk. : alk. paper) —
ISBN 978-0-87351-935-9 (ebook)
I. Brunot, Gudrun. II. Title.
PT9875.M5B713 2014
839.73'72—dc23
2013038932

This and other Minnesota Historical Society Press books are
available from popular e-book vendors.

The Brides of Midsummer

THE SPRING

I am water. I am the beginning. I was before the oaks, the grass, and the flowers. I was before the beasts that graze the grass. I was before hovering wing and scurrying foot. I was before the birds, the bees, and the bumblebees.

I was before sorrow and gladness. I was before the tears and the laughter. I was before the song, the music, and the dancing. I was before the torment, the suffering, and the anguish here on earth. I was before mankind.

From earth's darkest, innermost recesses flow my veins, known to no one. Yet, here, I surface at the foot of the hill. Here, I reflect the crowns of the oak trees and follow the generations of man throughout the world.

I am the spring. I am the beginning.

Time I

I, ANDERS ERIKSSON, OLD SPELMAN:*

Every Midsummer's Eve, I play my fiddle on the hill where the oak tree stands and where the villagers have raised their pole to see Midsummer's Day in. My place is inside this old hollow oak, where a board has been nailed up to serve as a seat for the spelman. Here I sit with my fiddle, deep within the ancientness of the rotting oak, playing so the young can dance.

For over forty years, I've played on Midsummer's Night at the oak hill. In my younger days, I would allow myself to act hard-to-get when they would ask me to bring my fiddle to play for them all through the night as they awaited Midsummer's Day. I was the only spelman then—there was no one else they could ask. Now, I get asked out of habit, and only at Midsummer. Other spelmen have cropped up, able to play other instruments. Now, it's the accordion they want. The fiddle is no longer the undisputed master. My

* The *spelman* was a key figure of rural village life, a player of traditional folk instruments, such as fiddle, accordion, harp. The spelman generally had no formal training and learned by ear from predecessors.—Tr.

fiddle is too old, my tunes are too old, I myself am too old now; I'm over sixty. There are younger spelmen. Now, all they want me for is to relieve some young stripling accordion player. So, once a year, at Midsummer, they'll put up with a bit of fiddling. I dare not play hard-to-get any more. I'm no longer indispensable. I am soon to be discarded, no longer the obvious king of the spelman's throne in the hollow oak tree.

Here on the hill of the oak tree, in our old cutting field, we have welcomed Midsummer for as long as anyone can remember. A better gathering spot than this haying field of ours is not to be found in our land. The soil is rich and fertile with all the flowers and grasses you could imagine, and all around stand the old oaks, forever unchanging as I've known them to be for as long as I've lived. These trees are stationary, patient, ponderous, slow to grow up and just as slow to wither. The same hollow wherein I sit and play tonight is where I used to crawl in as a boy for a game of hide and seek; that's how long the oak's old age lasts. And here, among the big oak trees, at the summit of the hill, the ground is even and flat, the floor spread there by God for the feet of the dancers. In the field at the bottom of the hill, there flows a spring where the dancers can drink their fill after working up a sweat and a thirst from their twirling. When I cease playing, and if people's merry-making stops for just one single moment, I can hear the purling of the spring.

Still, I'd rather take myself and my fiddle to other dances. Here, on the hill of the oak tree, I've never felt that real fiddler's joy. I've played at crossroads, in barns, at open-air dance floors and play-grounds, and experienced that perfect sense of everything working in harmony. But here, in our mowing field, my hands feel clumsy; the fiddle strings feel harsh and uncooperative. Maybe it's some-thing I'm imagining—I'm often fooled by my tendency to imagine things. Maybe the truth is that I simply know too much about this place. I know the truth about the soil where the young are dancing tonight. I know the secret of the hill with its oak tree.

It's my imagination that conjures up these pictures from the past before my eyes. The young know nothing, or wish to know nothing—they care nothing for stories that happened hundreds of years ago. I am about the only one to know about this place.

Though I know the secret of the hill and the oak tree, I come here once every year to play the night through. These days, this is the one and only time they'll want my playing. This is the bitter, humiliating truth—this is the only time of the whole round year when I get to play for the dancers. I've been trying to keep from admitting it to myself for as long as possible, but this is how things stand with old spelman Anders Eriksson.

It used to be a well-known fact that my fiddle made a good partner to the dancing. My tunes were treasured for their fine sense of rhythm. It's true I don't know many dance tunes: three waltzes, four polkas, three hambos, one shottish, and one polka-mazurka. But these tunes, I know them well, backward and forward. I'm so familiar with them that I can play them asleep in my bed. I learned these pieces as a boy; I played them better and better as time went on. I was comfortable with them, I entrenched myself in my tunes, and that's how I ended up not trying any new ones. And they will do for a whole evening of dancing—once I've played through all twelve of them, so much of the evening has gone by that I can simply strike up the waltz I started with and let the rest follow in the same order. And these pieces that I've played thousands of times, for thousands of dancing couples, played through my entire youth, as a grown man and now at the beginning of old age, they're named after me—this is Anders' waltz, Anders' hambo and Anders' polka. These tunes are well known; but people won't dance to them any more except on Midsummer's Eve. We have younger spelmen now.

At times, I'll simply play the tunes to myself. It happens when I sit in the dreary loneliness of my little cottage. And it's almost sure to happen when I've brought a liter of brandy home with me. And I play for no one but myself.

It's as green and lush now as ever here in our haying field in summer, and the night is as bright as it ever gets where we live. And with all this greenery, and with this daylight, the difference between youth and old age melts away before one's eyes. It's enough to make me wonder what old age is. I start wondering where the years are, my own years that are gone, and I wonder where are the years that will be. The leaves on the oak branches and the light from the sky that glows over them are ageless. The lush grass of the cutting field, soon to be mowed, is just like last year's grass, the year before that, and all the summers that passed before, they have no age. And the spring that runs down over the slope in its runnel, she has no age; she sings her water song as it has been sung all through time . . .

So, here I sit playing my fiddle on this board someone nailed up inside the oak that has no age, on this eternal Midsummer night. And I ask myself, how long have I been sitting here? I ask myself if it isn't for more than forty Midsummer nights, if I haven't been playing here for as long as the spring has kept tinkling and cascading her water down her furrow?

From up here in the oak tree, I have a good overview of fields and meadows. Over the green stripes of the field boundaries, the path runs up here to the hill, and between the squares with their tall rye and low oats, I see the stragglers, boys and girls, approaching on foot. The autumn rye is in full bloom and manhood at Midsummer, its ears giving off that smell somewhat reminiscent of a female in heat that drives men mad. Midsummer's Night is made pregnant with bread—bread steaming and ready for the ovens. Tonight, the rye is foaming.

I am playing my old dip waltz. It takes limber knees to dance it. That one isn't for those of us whose limbs have acquired the stiffness of old age, not for men like me. But in my younger years, I was considered a fairly nimble dance partner. At least, the girls told me I was a good leader. A good ear for rhythm is the hallmark of a spelman, that's like saying two and two makes four, but that doesn't always mean that one who can play is also a good dancer. I know some seasoned spelmen who can't take one step on the dance floor and simply would never be able to learn.

After the dip waltz, I want a sip from my flask. Inside my pocket, I grope for it. I've inherited it from my father. There is a flower painted on the glass of the flask—I'm not sure what kind it's supposed to represent—and below that, some printed words: "your health, my brother!" Those are comfortable, friendly words to see on a brandy flask—words of comradeship—they give you the feeling you're not drinking alone. They are good and welcome words for me, who almost always must drink alone—at least of late. As I uncork the flask, it's as if I saw my father open his long-bearded mouth and snort for the draft—that sound of contentment. I imagine that men who lived before him and perhaps drank from that same flask are with me in my little cottage as I take a swig. Through the years, I have derived much solace from what was inside the bottle, but those four words on the outside have brought me consolation as well.

I bring the flask to my mouth a few times. I greet all those who drank from it before me: "your health, my brother!"

My flask has already been refilled for this Midsummer watch. The brandy is my entire spelman's wages.

After the sip of brandy, I take some time tuning my fiddle. The strings are unwilling; I can't quite recognize them. They seem bent on not producing the sound I want, but a sound all their own. Maybe it's the night dampness that causes it.

Now, I'll play the piece that garnered me the most praise in my youth, the Bökevara Polka. I've named it after the village where I first heard it at a dance pavilion. In order to keep it in my head, I kept whistling it all the way home. I kept on whistling it until my chest grew quite ragged with exhaustion. Once I was home, I couldn't go to bed until I'd learned to play the new polka on my fiddle. I hadn't lost one single little bar of it; it was all there in my head. My playing woke up the whole house. Father got up and shouted and hollered and threatened. The way he was made, music was torture to him, be it from an accordion, a fiddle, a guitar, a pump organ or psalmodikon, he said it cut him like knives. But further back in time, there were supposedly spelmen in my family; I've been told we had one who played the fela,* as it was called then. At that hour before dawn, I was aware of nothing but the new polka. It was summer and, before I knew it, the sun poured in, gilding the dirty floor of my chamber with its glow. At last, Father came in and punched me hard a few times, making my earlobes smart and burn and my ears ring for days afterward. But I had learned that polka, there wasn't a glitch anywhere, I knew it from start to finish. By then, I was able to go to bed happy. I was in such good spirits that morning I can't remember ever feeling anything like it. My ears kept ringing and whooshing after Father's wallops, but inside my head, there played quite a different song.

* *Fela* or *lira*: a bowed string instrument where keys were struck to activate tangents which in turn served as frets. CF. *key harp*. —Tr.

The Bökevara Polka—oh, it can put some life back into any human body, be it ever so deeply buried in the mire of lumbering stodginess. With that polka, I believe my fiddle could move a skeleton to lift its bony knuckles, at least for an inch or so. It smarts the skin like the crack of a whip; it cracks like the whip itself. At the turn following the first repeat, it bursts into a driving, sizzling frenzy: *Crack! Crack!* Then, even the old folks standing around the walls watching the dancers can be seen moving their feet, then even the lame and crippled start stamping and wiggling their toes. There isn't a God-made man or woman who can bear to sit still then. Ah, with that polka, I have succeeded in playing many a young and lusty couple into exhaustion, dripping with sweat. Then, the couple might go outside to cool off, maybe to kiss and cuddle for a while. One or two young ones may have caught a chill afterward, maybe even pneumonia. My fiddle and the Bökevara Polka have, in all likelihood, been the death of some young lad or lass. It is all part of good dance music and the strange puzzle that makes up our lives. Oh, it is a fine polka, that one!

Sure enough, droplets of sweat are running down my forehead as I finish the Bökevara Polka and lower the fiddle from beneath my chin. The strings keep vibrating for quite a while afterward, though no bow is touching them. They tremble as if completely exhausted from driving the dancers round the maypole. Mine was the instrument that whipped the many couples round and round down in the grassy field. For a short while, the young ones in the prime of their growing have been forced into obeying my fiddle.

I take a few more swigs from my flask. I've already finished my own Midsummer brandy—I'm now drinking my spelman's wages. "Your health, my brother!"

My brothers always told me I was careless of myself and would, therefore, never reach old age. I never believed them.

I was the eldest of five children, but I was never drawn to farming, so our family homestead was given to my two youngest brothers to share. I built myself a small cottage on the least arable share of the land. That's where I've stayed ever since, earning my living from this and that. In our village, I am the man folks will hire for the odd jobs. I am skilled in such things that require delicate hands and a light touch. For my basic upkeep, a few things were given to me from my childhood home. I've suffered neither cold nor starvation. And whenever I could afford to, I sent for a liter of brandy.

They were right: I have been careless of myself, yet here I am, an old man. I'm sixty-three—I've become one of the aged. Still, my number of years makes up no more than one tenth of the age of the oak—of this tree that is my spelman's altar. The stem is rotted—yet from it new leaves will sprout long after I've rotted away in the earth. My own years I now see as a few brief moments that were at their fastest to run from me as I tried my hardest to keep them with me. In my childhood, the year was its own end; now barely has it begun than it's gone. Each New Year's Day brings me the same question: will this be the beginning of my last year?

And I, the old spelman, who mourns that I get to play for the dancers once a year only—here on the hill of the oak tree—I ask myself every Midsummer if this will be the last time.

The evening is wrapping its green darkness around us here at our watch. But there is light from above. And there, at the top of the hill, stands the pole.

Against the bright night sky strains the pole with long, outstretched arms. Each arm bears a wreath, made from the flowers the field offers. From the top of the pole, a birch branch sticks up like a cock's comb. The head of the pole resembles a raised cock's comb with sharp saw teeth. In earlier days, the top of the pole would sport a cock made from straw and we would shoot at it with small stones, trying to hit it. Barren women would put their arms around the maypole—for whatever good that did them—what would have been the use of attaching a straw cock at the top?

Our maypole stands on the hill tall as a giant, reaching his two arms high above our heads with flowers in his hands. His is the place of distinction at our vigil; he is the guest of honor tonight. Still, the maypole is a guest unknown, risen from the twilight depths of the past. Sitting here, I contemplate the scraggly cock's comb at its top, wondering where it came from.

Beneath me on the hill whirls the ring of dancers. Outside this moving circle, another circle has formed, though quite still. In this circle stand the girls that weren't asked to dance, the boys too shy to ask, those too young to dance, those no longer young enough. And over both human circles, the moving one and the still one, the old oaks stretch their dark, gnarly branches.

The scent of flowering rye fills the air and reaches my nose. Tonight, its smell is pregnant with summer in our land. It's my brothers' rye that's blooming, and its ears caressed my face, its chaff pricked my skin as I was crossing the field boundaries just a while ago. I halted, sniffed, sneezed, and inhaled the powerful mating scent of fecund rye.

On our hill and its surrounding field boundaries, there are more kinds of flowers growing than anyone can name. Here, the sage and lavender crowns lend their shades of blue; here, the spearmint sends out its fragrance; here, the grass is streaked with blue dress and star-of-Bethlehem, vetch and wolf's bane, crossvine and thyme. During haymaking, the flowers drop right into the hay to make up half of it. It's a sweet flower hay that gets raked up here within these fences. Should you lie down to rest in the barn where the hay is stored, you'd get dizzy from the smell.

Inside my little cottage, I have a few flowers that are more than two hundred years old. They have been painted on my clothes chest. On the front panel of this old blue chest, there are some red flowers glowing inside a ring. They say it used to be the custom to paint flowers on one's household utensils with one's thumb. Not that I'd know. But if the flowers on my clothes chest were painted there with someone's thumb, it's been skillfully done. I couldn't tell what sort of actual growing flowers they are supposed to be, but they glow with such a lifelike shine that I imagine I can almost smell them. The painter may have used his forefinger to help steady his strokes. Be that as it may, it's fine work.

The chest was once part of my share of the inheritance. In the middle, among the flower vines, the three letters "A. E. S." have been painted, plus the year "1711." A. E. S.—those are the initials of one of my forebears at the Högaskog homestead, Anders, Erik's Son. The man who painted flowers on his clothes chest in the year 1711 was my namesake. All he did different was to split up the surname into two words. Over two hundred years ago, there was my name on a clothes chest.

I think of him at times, Anders, Erik's Son. The flower he painted there, with or without the help of his thumb, is made up of the most peculiar and intricate scrollwork and it has the red-hot color of fire. I don't believe you could find that color among the flowers growing on the ground. I reckon Anders, Erik's Son, made it up himself one evening for lack of something better to do.

It was the year 1711. Two hundred years is a long time. But there are bound to be things that live outside of time and years. This Midsummer night, for example.

I keep pulling my pocket flask out between the tunes. Stroking those fiddle strings and driving the circle of dancers round and round is thirsty work. I think of Anders, Erik's Son, as I drink. Your health, my brother! What kind of man were you—you who painted those flowers on my clothes chest, those flowers that can't be found on this earth?

Soon, my playing for this evening will be done. Soon, I'll relinquish my place to the foremost spelman, the right spelman—the youth with the accordion. I never took the trouble to find out his name.

Compared to the voice of the fiddle, I must say I find the sound of the accordion harsh and without feeling—piercing, crude, and intrusive, the notes hard as iron and steel. Sure enough, their sound carries, but below the surface, they are of no consequence to me—to my soul, they do not matter. It's as though the accordion were without compassion. But the fiddle has its own entrails in its breast, a vulnerable heart that can tremble and throb with the suffering of other hearts. The strings of a fiddle come from living beings—that is undeniable. The sheep, that poor, dumb, sacrificial animal with its braying, the most off-putting of all animal sounds, carries the most delicate fiddle tones around in its wool-warmed belly.

I rosin my bow, grasp my slender fiddle around its waist, and strike up another dance tune:

"'Miss, a Shottish, a mazurka, or a waltz, what will it be?' Thanking you, kind sir, but dancing's not for me.'"

It's my only Shottish. It bounces like a lightly sprung wagon on a bumpy country lane. It is rather whimsical.

I play, drink some, play again.

But each Midsummer night that I've been sitting here, I've been telling myself: you who know the secret of the hill ought not to play at dances up here. You ought to keep in mind what kind of place this is.

But the Midsummer watch has been observed from year to year here for as long as those now living can remember and nothing has happened. And what could possibly happen? No enlightened person could get the idea that we'd be disturbed here on Midsummer's Night. I'd think we would be seen as the disturbers with our playing and dancing.

I sit here on my elevated spelman's seat and watch the circle of dancers billow back and forth beneath me. These are the young ones, expending their excess vigor, charging around in their happiness, in the happiness of their sweet, blessed oblivion. No one broods over the old stories about the oak hill; no one remembers them while the dancing goes on. Every foot is lifted lightly over this soil that hides the past, all sunken away, all forgotten. I might be the only one to sit here and remember. I have no doubts; I know these aren't imaginings and old wives' tales, but God's truth. And I'll never be able to forget it:

The dancers are twirling over human graves. It's a burial ground we've chosen for our Midsummer's Eve dancing. These young, giddy couples are using the resting places of the dead for their merriment:

I sit here, playing in a churchyard.

My memory of the first time I heard about it is hazy and unclear— once, way back, the plague ran rampant here, killing all the people with the exception of an old woman and a child. There were so many corpses that it became impossible to bury them all in the parish cemetery. New burial grounds were inspected and established in the outlying lands, in meadows and enclosed pastures near the homesteads. Somewhere here in this very meadow where we mowed our grass and gathered our hay in the summer time, one such burial ground is said to have been situated. Twenty plague victims are said to lie buried there.

I heard many tales told by old men and women when I was a child, and, for me, this became just one tale among others. I heard how plague sufferers went and dug their own graves, and when they felt the hour of death draw near, they'd go and lie down in them, so as not to run the risk of being left unburied. There simply weren't enough survivors to bury them. Those were the sort of things supposed to have happened according to these stories.

Many years went by, and I was well into my adult years when a stranger walked into my cottage one day. He was clad as a gentleman in a white straw hat and a suit of soft, fine cloth, and on his feet he wore shining, well-polished buttoned boots. He was some sort of lecturer, a learned man, a researcher of the past. He was going from one part of the country to another, recording peculiar happenings from times gone by. Now, he was working on a book, or article, or whatever he called it, about a devastating plague that struck Sweden and all the North countries during the reign of Karl XII.* He already had written records of all the plague victims of every parish around here. He showed me his notes—ours had been hit harder than any other parish in the county—approximately half the resident population had died from the disease.

This was a strange fact for me to learn. This time, however, the lecturer was busy gathering facts about the locations in the surrounding areas where the plague victims had been buried. Our parson had told him facts that brought him to my family homestead and its property. Someone had hinted to him that I might know a thing or two about the place, since this was the home of my birth.

Hearing this, all the old stories about our cutting field flooded back into my memory. I brought the stranger to the area—the spot ought to be somewhere here within this fenced-in pasture. And it

* Charles XII, 1682–1718, king of Sweden, 1697–1718.—Tr.

wasn't long before the stranger had located the right spot. This hill,* the oak hill, was the place he sought.

The researcher pointed to a couple of stones, arranged in even rows that could be seen protruding from the soil border. I've been seeing these stones for years; I'd come here with my scythe to mow and cut the grass in between them. Never had it occurred to me even once that they formed the boundary of a cemetery. These were the remnants of a wall that had been erected there to mark the resting place of those who had died from the plague. Over time, the wall had crumbled and collapsed, later to be removed, piece by piece, by people who were ignorant of why it had originally been built there. Thus, the centuries had marched on, covering other cemeteries from times of human decimation with the grass of oblivion. Nobody was alive here anymore that would be able to point out the graves.

The professor in his white straw hat and his shining button boots paced out the plague cemetery in our meadow: thirty-two paces one way, sixteen paces the other way. I got thirty and fifteen, having longer legs than the learned gentleman. The spot was certainly large enough for twenty people, he said. There were probably even more people buried within the shelter of these stones.

The professor referred to the hill with the old oak trees as a remarkable historic monument.

After his visit, I began mulling over whether it wouldn't be seen as unbefitting for me to keep on striking up dance tunes for the vigil on the oak hill. It was a final resting place after all, though overgrown and forgotten. But Midsummer had been danced over

---

* OT Hult, "Sweden under the plague 1710 relates the account of the County Governor of Kronoberg: the figures on the parish of Algutsboda page 143: infected homesteads 67, number of parishioners dead from the plague 663."—Au.

people's graves one year after the other, and the dead had never shown any signs of discontentment. Nothing ever happened that might be perceived as a reason for halting the merrymaking of the young. That was perhaps largely due to the dying off of all the old folks that were able to hear and observe supernatural things. Younger people didn't believe in any ghosts. Except for the one or two foolish folks that think the dead can harm the living, the rest of us know we are as unreachable to the dead as they are to us.

So I continued to play at the Midsummer watch, though no longer with the same, unspoiled joy as I used to. From that time on, I'd be constantly making excuses, telling myself over and over that I wasn't disturbing the peace of the dead with my fiddle. Were I still able to retain some connection with the living after my death—so I told myself—I would have no objection to a bit of playing and dancing over my grave. No, I wouldn't mind; on the contrary, I'd welcome hearing some ditties from the earth above; at least once a year, on Midsummer's Eve, I'd like it very much. Were I to hear any of the ones I used to play, I'd be twice as happy down there in my grave. It would gladden my heart to know that the young still had sense enough to amuse themselves. The young couples would have my blessing to do as they pleased on my grave. I would take no offense if they got as near to one another as they possibly could, if they chose to lie together on my resting place. Quite the opposite: it would be a tribute to an old fiddler whose music brought many a young body to fever and frenzy, who may have earned part of the blame for the case of adultery, as the law will call it. Yes, the young couple would honor me better with their lovemaking than if they laid flowers upon my grave.

Hadn't I myself experienced a thing or two at this old burial ground? Here, on this hill, I had my first girl. It happened before I knew the spot was a cemetery. I didn't deliberately choose this spot.

Here, a girl lost her virginity to me on a Midsummer's Night. Actually, it was almost morning when it happened: the sun was already shining on the red spots that had appeared on a clover bush. Or, maybe on the vetch leaves or on a lily of the valley. I can't remember for certain—it's forty-five years ago—but it seems to me that these drops of blood lay on some wild clover leaves.

It wasn't intended in any way; it just happened. Ellen was seventeen; I was eighteen. We were equally awkward, inarticulate, shy, and hot with our fumbling hands. Neither of us had done it before, neither of us would afterward have been able to say how it came to happen. It just happened: all of a sudden, we'd been near one another. I'd almost say we couldn't help it. We wanted it, but we wouldn't have dared, had we thought of it. We didn't have the courage to do it. We must have had help from someone or something, or it wouldn't have happened. It was as though someone had grasped us and laid us down in the grass. On our own, we would never have dared to do it. No, not even today do I understand how it happened, how we managed.

From what I can remember, I didn't get much pleasure from what we did, but afterward, I was glad and contented anyhow. After all, I had been the first with Ellen. She'd given me the maiden's treasure, as it used to be called, the most precious thing she owned, a girl's most valued asset second to her dowry. That was some gift for a boy like me. It meant Ellen must be fond of me. Why else would she give up her maiden's treasure to me? No, that is not something a girl gives away without feeling serious liking for a boy. So, I certainly had reason to be glad.

Ellen had whimpered a little at first, like a child in its sleep, for they say it hurts when that path is broken. But toward the end, she murmured something unintelligible in my ear, and it didn't sound like whimpers of pain. Then, she grew quite silent. She lay there without making a sound for a long time, and I didn't say much either. We were both overwhelmed by what we'd just done, speechless by the thought of what we'd just dared. We were terrified and proud at the same time. In all likelihood, I was the one to feel mostly proud, Ellen the one to feel mainly terrified. We had been such innocent children. Now, as an experiment, we had suddenly graduated out of the clothes of innocence. Maybe the thought that we would never again be able to put them on made us anxious. Ellen was more troubled over it than I was. I believe she was more strongly affected by what had just happened. It's understandable—there's a change that takes place in a girl's body the first time, she loses something.

Ellen was first to get up: she said she'd walk down to the spring to wash in its running water. Initially, I placed no significance in her wishing to go and wash herself. But then, she added:

"I've heard it will work—now, on Midsummer's Night."

Judging from her arch look as she uttered these words, she seemed to be hinting at some secret she mustn't tell. That's when I began to wonder what she could mean. What good would it do to wash in the meadow spring and nowhere else? It didn't make any sense to me right away.

Ellen stayed away for quite a while down the hill by the spring. I couldn't tell what she was up to, probably exactly what she'd said she'd be up to. Still, I had the feeling there was something mysterious in what she was doing. Her errand at the spring must have something to do with what had just occurred between us.

I wondered if it would be stupid of me to ask; as a teenager, one is naturally afraid of saying or doing anything that might be construed by others as a sign of stupidity, but when Ellen came back, I asked her anyway:

"Why is it such a good thing for you to wash in the spring on this night?"

We weren't going to mention it again, was her answer.

I left it at that. I had touched on something she couldn't talk about with me. There wasn't anything for me to do but drop the subject.

The sun was shining, and on the ground where we'd lain, the red drops of blood glistened on the leaves of the clover blossom. I'd read about sacrificial blood in the bible, and sacrificial blood is what this made me think of. The sacrifice had been made to me. I was happy and contented, and there was something solemn about that happiness that bordered on religious devotion.

At that time, I didn't know that the blood-speckled clover was growing on human graves. Later, the thought occurred to me that life and death had been very closely intertwined that morning.

From then on, Ellen and I got together on several occasions, almost as awkwardly as the first time. For a few years, we were a couple.

Thirty-five years ago, however, Ellen got married to a rich farmer. Nowadays, she's a jolly farmer's wife, going to fat, with six grown children. I'm always welcome in her home, however. She's always quick to put the coffee pot on the stove. She's very kind to me. Maybe her kindness comes out of relief that she never got pregnant and had to marry me. Ellen must be thankful not to have become my wife, since I behaved so shamefully a few years after that Midsummer's Night. No man in our village has behaved more despicably than I, Anders Eriksson of Högaskog. No other man in our village ever went to jail. But Ellen remained just as kind to me after my time in jail as before. I think she still likes me a little even now, even though she was wise enough to choose a better husband for herself than I would have been.

I feel a secret sense of superiority toward Ellen's husband. Whenever I see him, I think: "I was with her first. You came second! You may be ever so rich, but you got to make do with second place." And with the strong sons and beautiful daughters of the house, I feel somehow related. They are not children of mine, but it's Ellen, my first girl, who gave birth to them. It's as if I were the one to unlock the door for them into this life.

Ellen has given birth to beautiful daughters, that's a fact, and the most beautiful one is here on the oak hill this evening—I just caught sight of her within the circle around the pole. A tall, bareheaded girl with shining, blond hair, it's Gertrud, the youngest. No man can help noticing her and watching her with interest. I feast my eyes on her for as long as I can, every time I meet her on the road. This girl is created such that I can't do otherwise. Then, I also believe that Gertrud is of the same sweet and gentle nature as her mother.

Yes, it's forty-five years since that Midsummer I lay here with Gertrud's mother. Still, one question has remained unanswered for all these years between Ellen and me: Why would it be helpful for a girl to wash in the meadow spring on the oak hill at Midsummer? I never learned the answer to that one. Still, forty-five years later, I wonder about it now and then.

Our watch has been going on for quite a while. The fiddle's time will be up soon, and the accordion will take its place. The rightful spelman will take my place on the seat within the hollow oak. But there are still a few tunes I really want to play before I go from here. After all, this is the only time these days that I get to sit on my old spelman's throne, high above all the people. And I don't know if I'll be back here next year. A lot can happen in a year: people die at my age, and I'm obviously not as well as I used to be. So I want to play these last few tunes.

The truth is, this is my best moment of the whole year. The truth is that I'd rather not leave from here at all.

I pull out the flask again, there are only a few drafts left in it, let them go! Your health, my brother! So, now, I've drunk my entire spelman's wages for this Midsummer. My brandy flask is empty again, as it is most of the time. I'd like to see a flask that, for six days of the week, is emptier than mine. And I'm sober once more, as I am most of the time. My brothers who own my childhood home say I'm well on my way to boozing myself to death. But they've been saying and repeating that year-round for thirty-five years, which goes to show how much truth there is in it.

I've always felt such great pity for my brothers. They are anxious men, and anxious people are the most unfortunate of all. My brothers worry about their children, about the farm. They worry about the people who work for them and they worry about their beasts. Come spring, they worry about whether they'll get their sowing done in time; come summer, they fret about whether the seeds will have enough time to ripen; come autumn, they're afraid there won't be enough time for the harvesting. But most of all, they worry about dying. Now, they have reached a stage in their lives of well-being, of relative security; and now, they're getting older; now, they'll soon be dead. I feel sorry for my brothers, I always have.

I thought about death quite often in my youth. Then, I didn't ever want to get older than thirty, thirty-five at the most. Death was preferable to becoming an old man. I became an old man anyhow, yet I'm still alive. And now, I don't want to die for anything in the world. Now, I want to live, live forever and ever. Not because I'm more afraid of dying than I was when I was young, but because I've lost my fear of living. I've become truly accustomed to living by now, after having struggled with it for so long. I know its devilishness, its cunning; I know there isn't really anything you can cling to

or trust. But I've begun to get used to it, that's why I don't want
to die. Still, death comes a little bit closer to me with each breath I
take. I ought to have been happy in my youth, when I had it at such
a distance. But I was far from happy, and I had no idea of how close
or far away death was. What I wonder most these days is: in what
way will it come? What will it feel like? Will it be cruel or merciful
to me? Will I have a long, painful time of dying in a sickbed, or
will I die quickly and easily? Will I be tortured for a long time
beforehand, or will it be so quick that I'll never grasp or understand
what is happening? Death behaves so differently toward different
people. The one may lie in agony for years before he dies, while the
other escapes the suffering altogether. Death is rather unfair in
that sense; there is much talk about people being equal nowadays,
but in this case, there is no such thing as equality. Where will it
seize me when my time comes? In my liver, in my lungs, in my kid-
neys, in my stomach, in my heart, in my head? Death has so many
excellent, vulnerable entries into the human body to choose from,
way too many. Like a heart, for example, mine or someone else's
fragile heart . . .

But it's damn foolishness to be brooding over such things here
tonight at the spelman's seat! Enough of that!

I wish someone would come and refill my brandy flask. If they'd
only raise my spelman's wages! I have been playing Midsummer for
forty years: I deserve a raise.

I can see my nephews in the circle of dancers. I need have no
concern over the health of our family tree and its number of off-
shoots. My brothers have seen to that. Their sons have already
reached the age when the body becomes unruly in the company of
women. I just caught sight of my oldest nephew luring a girl into
the bushes. He's quite eager for girls, that boy. The peculiar fact
that has remained since the olden days is that a girl who may have

been guarding her treasure until now is likely to let go of it on Midsummer's Night. One or two maidenheads will be sacrificed in this meadow tonight. My nephews are getting ready to add yet another generation to our family tree.

Several times, they've been passing by the oak tree, but they pretend not to have noticed their uncle. My brothers have instilled no regard for me in their sons. They've instilled quite different ideas in them. Countless times, they've repeated the same to their boys: Take care not to become like your uncle Anders! Regard sprung from such admonishments would be a rare thing indeed! My nephews are ashamed of their uncle. Having a relative like me is no pleasure, I must, for the sake of honesty, admit that to myself. It ought to be possible to select one's relatives. But if we were fortunate enough in this world for this to be the case, neither my brothers nor my nephews would have selected me, that, I would stake my fiddle on.

And I have no right to bear them grudge for this. No one would be quick to select a jailbird as his brother or uncle.

About my going to jail—there's jail and there's jail. One could say I committed a crime, or one could say my thoughtlessness and carelessness led to an accident. You can earn yourself a few years in jail in one single moment—a brawl and a punch that hits too hard. That's all it takes. And there you are, locked up for years without end, turning it over and over in your mind—one rash moment and the facts that added their sad, unfortunate momentum. The other brawlers also wielded objects to fight with and hit even harder. But they did not go to jail. Their punches struck parts of the body that could withstand them. But my punch—my single punch—struck someone's thin, fragile temple.

My right hand that now holds the bow of my fiddle has never been a particularly powerful hand, but it has caused another person's

death. Nothing did I wish for less than what happened in that
moment, nothing in my life seems less understandable than this
death I caused.

A comrade throws you an insult. You retaliate with a stone. You
get drunk, get mad, you pick up a stone from the ground and throw
it. That's all it takes: involuntary manslaughter, grievous maltreat-
ment leading to another man's death. The county court officials all
had different names for it. Everyone thought my punishment was
mild. Some of it I never served since I was such a good prisoner.
But I lost two summers of my life. For two summers, I was never
allowed to stretch myself out in my full length in the soft grass.
And there were two Midsummers when I didn't get to play at the
oak hill.

My whole life would have turned out different had I not picked
up and thrown that stone as a young lad. I was only twenty-one
when I did it. After that, everything went to pieces for me. I had
been getting along fine with Ellen; we'd been talking about mar-
riage and finding ourselves a small homestead. But then, I threw
that stone and it all went to pieces. I don't blame Ellen. Jail is jail,
never to be forgotten. It still isn't, more than forty years later. Suddenly, someone will remember and toss out a casual word. Nothing
in this world can remove that dirt stain from me. It has contaminated those born of the same woman as I. My brothers get their
share now and then—how tragic, that thing with Anders—and
then, they're ashamed of me, my worthy brothers.

It's still rolling, that stone I threw. It's kept rolling in my footsteps
for more than forty years. It's been rolling in my footsteps ever since
that evening when I'd just turned twenty-one.

It was the accursed work of one moment. Sure, one can blame
the drinking. But it doesn't settle the matter of who is guilty, not
by any stretch of the imagination. What made me drink until I was

intoxicated? I didn't want to drink until I reached that stage. I never wanted to; I never really wanted to drink. And yet, I've done it, am still doing it, I'm sitting here drinking this evening. For in the long run, I can't stand it if I don't. Why was I made so that I do things I don't want to? Even when stone-cold sober, I've done what I've regretted thousands of times—I've flown into a temper, hurt and offended people deeply, uttered words I'd give anything to have unsaid again. It wasn't possible to blame the booze in those instances. No, the fact is that I constantly carry this thing inside me that forces me to commit the evil deed of a moment, what I do not want. There is some force within me—how many times haven't I raged against it in my regret, cursed it, wished it to hell. That force has been the never-ending plague of my life. It's caused me regret, and regret has been my lifelong curse.

Why does man do what he doesn't want? The one who comes up with an answer to that question would solve many of the riddles that confuse life on this earth.

It's been my miserable fate to cause disaster in one single moment and spend the rest of my life regretting it. Imagine throwing a stone at twenty-one and finding it rolling along behind you at sixty-three!

Is it any wonder, then, that my good brothers have taught their sons to be ashamed of me? I'd say it's just as well I don't have a son of my own. But down there in the wide circle of dancers, I see a bareheaded, blond girl, Ellen's youngest daughter. I feel as though this girl, Gertrud, were more of my kin than my nephews. She would have been born regardless of me, but still, I was the first to be with her mother. She once lay in Ellen's womb, and that is what I feel is creating a bond between us.

Gertrud's gaze is open and trusting, her eyes both dancing and gentle. That girl's nature is soft and sweet. If I were a relative of hers, I don't think she would be ashamed of me.

It's been ten years or so since I was last near a woman. Now and then, I feel a man's yearning, but more and more time goes by between such stirrings. I have perhaps become weaned of such cravings. No doubt that's what happens over time, when one lives alone as I do. But I am not blind, my eyesight is keen, so I see that there are still handsome lasses growing up in this world. I cannot help watching them. And the damned thing is that I'll watch them and have to be satisfied with just watching.

"The accordion! The accordion!"

Someone is shouting for the second spelman, or rather, for the first one, the right one. People are beginning to grow tired of the fiddle and the old tunes. But I'll be damned if I let them talk me out of playing those last few tunes before I step down from my spelman's throne. Who knows if I'll ever get to ascend it again? For a little while yet, the bow will glide over my strings, and the young people will just have to put up with my fiddle for a little bit longer. I've got a fine waltz that I haven't played this evening, and a hambo that's no piece of crap either.

Sing, my fiddle! Ring around, my dancing circle! Anders Eriksson of Högaskog is playing still.

"The accordion! Bring the accordion!"

The swine! Can't keep silent, can they! Throats for screaming, that's something the young people of our time have been provided with in spades. But they can't show any respect for those who have been part of this world much longer than they have and know a thing or two about it. I pretend not to hear those loudmouths. I remain seated here, playing. I will move away from here of my own free will only, not at the command of some sniveling whelp who thinks he's got the right to make himself heard just because he's young and because no one else has ever been young. Such pink little piglets! But I sit here, elevated above them all, once a year, and this is it, my great, longingly anticipated night, my night of exaltation. So I remain seated.

My throat is parched and hot like a warmed-up baking oven. I glance at my empty brandy flask, and she cries her scorn at me: your health, my brother! I want a refill. Don't I have the right to demand a raise of my spelman's wages after all the years I've served?

I catch the attention of a couple of lads standing down below and explain to them my heart's desire. A kind soul climbs up to me on the spelman's throne and hands me his pocket flask. "Keep it," he says. "Your health, my good young brother," I say.

"Don't give the old geezer any more brandy."

"Be quiet! Be quiet . . . !"

"But he's already had enough to drink."

The words were said quietly, almost in a whisper, but I heard them. And I recognized the voice of my eldest nephew. It didn't surprise me in the least: my nephew wants to deny me the well-deserved wages for my spelman's work. That's just like my family. Haven't I earned this flask of brandy after all the summers I've sat here and played? Forty Midsummers, that's how many I've played here. Isn't that enough, my dear nephew?

Well, it's true; I was away for two summers in a row. Those two Midsummers I spent sitting on a low stool in a small, small room looking at four grey-white walls. I knew these four walls backward and forward by then. I knew their every stain; every crack in their grey-white dullness was all too familiar to me. I had been staring at them for hours aplenty. I'd had all the time in the world to transform these spots into green islands in a desolate sea, I'd turned the cracks into rivers, their waters foaming their course through flower-filled pasturelands and fenced grassy fields. The only way I could have borne these four grey-white walls was to transform them. In jail, you have lots of time to accomplish things. The night where I should rightfully have been playing my fiddle on the oak hill, I spent seated on the stool within those four walls, swearing and crying. I swore at the jail that held me and cried over this my character trait that forced me to do what I didn't want to do, what I never wanted to do.

I've done a lot of swearing and crying in my life. I doubt there are many people on this earth who have cursed and cried as much as I have. Some people have considered me a roughneck and a drunkard, and they were right. Some have referred to me as a harmless poor fellow, and they, too, have been right. I am the crude cusser and drinker; I am the harmless, blubbering old spelman Anders Eriksson. That is all I know. It isn't much, almost nothing, about myself that I know.

Now I don't give a damn about these loudmouths and their calls for the other spelman. After my release from jail, I was asked to play at the Midsummer watch as usual; maybe because they had no other spelman in those days, but it still felt as though a brotherly hand stretched out to the disgraced, it was a form of restitution. And that restitution has been mine every year ever since. Once a year, Anders Eriksson gets to be heard and sit at the place of honor. And now, I don't want to relinquish that place to anyone else. This is my night of glory.

I empty the new flask and keep on playing: the dancing goes on in the cemetery.

Many times, I've been coming up here on the hill alone to think about the human graves from the days of Karl XII. Peace reigns here, and quiet, at all times of the year except for Midsummer's Night. The old oaks stand rotting away in their hollow ancientness, but they will not fall. They still flourish from all their gaping holes and all the bumps and gnarly growths on their trunks. The noble old torsos are covered by skin resembling that of an old man—gnarled and wrinkled, and their branch-limbs are swollen with knotted varicose veins. Yet, undaunted by wounds and signs of aging, they still send out their yearly profusion of leaves. Here, the noble oak species is represented by some stately old grandfathers.

Early spring is the prettiest time here when the wood anemones cover the ground. The anemone plants in their profusion quite cover the plague cemetery like sheets, spread out to dry and whiten in the sun. Then, one is loath to walk and tread on the hill, for fear of trampling all this new growth, so fragile and delicate. Later, in the middle of summer, the scent of cumin and ripe herbs is redolent, and the drone of the bumblebees can be heard from the dwellings of the grass roots like rumbling music from underground, a melodious organ music played by the dead. But in the summer time, there is nothing here to remind one of death; no, everything is alive, every blade of grass, every insect is alive and thriving. In the autumn, when the meadow has been grazed by the cattle, all is different. The plague cemetery lies there then, naked and violated, manure-speckled, its soil stirred up by hooves. There is nothing beautiful about this spot then. As autumn goes on to spread the dry, crackling oaken leaves, the long, wearying dreariness sets in. All that meets the eye, then, is a poignant sense of desolation. One would imagine that even the dead are bored and find their time exceedingly cheerless where they are.

We humans can count our years of living, but we do not know the years of the soil. The soil has no age. It has experienced and known much, but it doesn't get old. I've done some reading about the history of this land of ours, and this is what I have been thinking: how the use of a patch of land can shift in the time of a thousand years, from a gathering place to honor the gods or send a man to the gallows, for the young to sport and play, for lowering a loved one into his grave. Consequently, the thought occurs to me that the oak hill has been biding here, fertile with the past, weighed down by all it has seen through the ages. What hasn't it witnessed from the beginning of earth's creation until this day? This spot must be saturated with secrets that no one can unveil.

One thing I know for certain—this is the place of the rested ones. Only someone who has died gets to remain forever in one spot.

And I can sit here wondering: what kind of people were those who died of the plague who have been decomposing down here? What did they get out of life? Were they forebears of mine, any of them? If so, was this relative like me in any way, as far as appearance, mannerisms, or temperament?

One can always wonder. In a book I read in jail—in jail, that's where I started reading books and had the leisure to ponder the peculiarities of human life—I found these words that I've never forgotten: "To live is to ask. To die is to find the answer." Does it then follow that those twenty who vanished into the ground on this hill got their answers? Hell knows.

What will death have to tell us? Best not to put too much trust in those words. Maybe there'll be no answer. Death, well, I'm picturing it like a gun barrel aimed at me, a long barrel that can reach across the entire earth. Wherever I am, whatever position I am in, whatever I do, the end of that barrel is aimed at my body. Death is aiming, but that's all for now; it has me in its sight. One day, the shot will go off, nobody knows when, so the only thing I know for sure is that there'll be a bang. I'd imagine death is aiming at my heart. It's started behaving so strangely these last few years, it's begun skipping in my chest: it's as if the hollow where the heart lies were too small and shallow for it. All of a sudden, without any exertion whatsoever on my part, my heart will start heaving and dancing around in there. It's a sprightliness that doesn't quite appeal to me . . . it makes breathing quite difficult. I haven't gotten around to seeing a doctor about it. Truth to tell, I've never had the money to seek medical help for anything. I'll take a sip of brandy as soon as the heart starts jumping: that calms it down, at least for a little while.

Play, my fiddle! Dance, my couples! I've got one more piece to play for you. It's as dark now as it ever gets here in the mowing field at Midsummer. In the dark, I can see the maypole rise like a primitive giant, broad-shouldered with thick arms covered with green, lush hair, a giant with a cock's comb on his head.

And if I listen closely and stop playing, I can hear a quiet purl reach me from the hill below—the voice of the spring. Through the hubbub of human voices, I can, for a brief moment, hear the coursing of the spring.

This is a spring that runs north. It is peculiar: I know of no other spring that runs north. And this is a spring that never runs dry. During dry summers, when many wells are empty, we can fetch water from this our meadow spring. In the difficult and arid summer of 1906, the entire village collected water in horse-drawn wagons from the oak hill, filling barrels, buckets, kettles, and pots. Every evening, the spring was emptied, and every morning, it was full to the brim once more. It filled us all with wonder. The spring is like a human being: tired and beat at night, resting and gathering strength while sleeping, to act with fully restored power come morning. The human being will be used up one day, however; the spring will never be. She is an eternal well.

The spring is the one to give us our lush hay here. It nourishes the meadow with its water, flooding its furrow out over the ground in the autumn and spring. The more it overflows in the spring, the more hay we can harvest in the summer. The water from the spring turns the entire meadow rich and fertile. Within this small circumference grow raspberries and hazelnuts, rosehips as well as wild apples, hops as well as wintergreen, rowanberries as well as whitebeam. As a matter of fact, our meadow is said to hold all manner of foliferous trees. That's how strong the growth is that is nourished by this spring. Were it to run dry, our soil would dry out. It is indispensable to us.

The water is clear like a child's gaze, absolutely transparent. Once when the villagers had cleaned the spring out, an old silver coin was found at the bottom of it. There was no stamp on the coin to indicate its age, but it was certainly hundreds of years old. There was more digging through the mud at the bottom of it, and two more coins were found. It's a most peculiar spring.

It's been running here since the day this green earth was created, giving the richness of water, entire seas of water. And yet, it's no more than a few meters deep. If you lean down over it, you can see the bottom. But it's sure to have another bottom, one that's deeper down, one that has never been seen by anyone.

I often stop here to listen to the song of the spring, try to interpret it. Now, I'm listening again after the last echoing note from the fiddle, and, suddenly, I hear it: it's what I've been fearing. Now, I know, I hear it in the mumbling from the spring:

This is your last time, your very last time. Never again shall you play at the watch, Anders Eriksson! The premonition I've been feeling all evening will come true.

The dancers are getting more and more dissatisfied and giving voice to their complaints. Do they think I can't hear them: "Why doesn't anybody shoo the old man away with his fiddle so the right spelman can take his place? For a little while, one can put up with the old tunes at Midsummer, but they've been going on way too long."

They want to depose me from my spelman's throne.

Never have I forced my playing on anyone. The whole year, I keep my strings to myself. If, for this one time a year, they are to sound for other ears, I want my say as to how long they shall be sounding. And I know it now: I'll be finished up here after tonight. Forever. That's why I'm staying. There's still a bit to drink left in the flask they gave me.

"Don't give the old man any more! Can't you see he's soused!"

So, that's what you think, my dear nephew! Huh! Don't think I didn't hear you! Anyone who begrudges the spelman his wages, I want to meet man to man.

Here, I'm finishing the second flask as well. And now, by God, I'll play again! I'll unleash all that's hidden in the secret depths of my fiddle. The right energy has seized me now. Now, I breathe with a new, young chest. May the devil take 'em, there'll be music tonight at the oak hill! I'll strike up my dance tunes so that the dead can hear it down there under the grass where they were buried such a long time ago. For the cascading notes from the spring have told me: it's the very last time. Never more shall I be invited back here again to my rightful place, elevated, to be spelman of all the people. This is my last night of restitution.

So I stay put.

Here comes a young lad lumbering up to me in the oak, and he carries a big accordion on his back. I don't remember his name, but it makes no difference. It's the other spelman, the first one, the right one, the foremost one. He's a tall, raw-boned youth. Broad shoulders, broad chest, broad back, legs spread apart, broad mouth, everything about him is broad. With me, all is narrow, my shoulders, my chest, and my back.

He takes up a lot of room, that broad youth, up here in the narrow oak chamber. The spelman's seat is narrow; there isn't room for more than one here. There isn't room for anyone but me.

The other one stands there, waiting for me to get up. I remain seated.

"That's enough now," he says.

"Is that so," I reply.

No matter how "enough" it is, my playing, I'm not through yet.

"That's enough now," says the raw-boned youth in a louder voice.

"Think so, huh," I reply.

That's what he thinks, right. And if I am not of the same mind? He is young. There will be many times for him to play. But I'm old, and I'll never get to come back to this my rightful place again. Never again—those are words to think about. I, who have played here for more than forty years, should I be chased off by some broad-snouted whelp of a lad who thinks he's just going to stalk up here and say: That's enough now! I won't have it. I'm staying.

They are hollering and screaming down there, the dancers. They are impatient. They want to drive me off, the bastards. They want to rob me of my night of restitution, my last one. They humiliate an old spelman who has sat here scratching his fiddle, the servant of youthful gaiety for more than one generation. I'm not getting up.

A girl climbs nimbly up to us in the oak grotto. It's Gertrud, Ellen's daughter. My first sweetheart's youngest, her prettiest daughter.

She has eyes that glisten like dew on grass, they shine in the dark night, her cheeks are hot from dancing, her breasts move up and down under the cloth of her dress. Gertrud is totally immersed in the pleasure of this night's dancing; she is rushed and gasping. The girl's entire body is lusting for dancing, dancing, and more dancing.

"Uncle Anders, thank you so much for this evening," she says.

Then, she takes my hand to draw me up from the spelman's seat.

"Come with me, Uncle Anders!"

The touch of the girl's hand affects me in a peculiar way, and the effect is immediate. The soft-skinned, fevered hand of a woman, awkward like a child's, somewhat damp with sweat, has grasped my hand. And that is all it takes to stir my entire, age-ridden body.

Ten years it is since the last time. I've almost forgotten what it's like to be with a woman. But now, all at once, it comes storming back through my body. It washes over me, shoots through me from head to toe like searing pain.

"Be good now, Uncle Anders. Come with me."

Gertrud, Ellen's daughter, clasps my hand tightly, drags at my hand. She has probably been delegated by the others to come up here and try to get me away from here and leave my place to the other one. The old man is drunk, he's being refractory; let's send a girl up there to coax some sense into him. But I'm no old man. I have got a new, young breast and young, strong hands. I am not old; I have strength in my arms yet. Now, at the touch of a young girl's warm hand, I realize what a powerful body I still have.

Gertrud wants me to follow her down. I'll come with her all right. But on one condition.

I grasp the girl around her waist, soundly; I feel the girlish breasts like soft, downy nestlings under the cloth of her dress. The breasts yield and give with the pressure of my fingers. It stirs me, as if a storm were raging through my body. I seize the girl's breasts, hard, fiercely.

And then I say the words.

What came over me? I heard my own voice; I could hear what I said, quite distinctly. There's no denying it: the words came out of my own mouth.

What madness! How could I say it? And in the presence of other people to boot? I mean, anyone who could say such a thing to a girl, whether or not anyone else is listening, must be a person with no sense of shame. But it was me and nobody else who said it:

"Can I sleep with you? I'll go with you then."

That's how I spoke to Gertrud when she asked me to come down with her. And it was my mouth that uttered the most insane words. It was my mouth that added:

"I lay here with your mother once. I'd rather stick with the family."

No! No! Could I have been the one to say those last words? No! No! Someone else must have been speaking, imitating my voice. Merciful lord and all the devils, it couldn't have been me, could it?

"Let go! Oh, God, let go of me!"

She shrieks, piercingly, at the top of her voice.

Gone is the merry gleam from Gertrud's eyes. The girl's face is all horror and revulsion now. I've let go of her hand. But she doesn't release my hand, but flings it from her, hurls it as far away from her as she can, with all her strength. Her mouth gapes open in horror.

"Let go of me!"

She says nothing more but stands silent, her muteness exorcizing me.

The girl throws my hand from her and hurries down.

The touch of her hand has shown me that man's yearning is not as yet extinguished in me. It bubbled up and washed through me like in earlier times. I suppose it nothing but feeble old man's lust. I wasn't seeking anything from the girl. I swear I wasn't. The mere thought would be the clearest, sheerest madness. So why did I speak it? What took hold of my judgment so that I let this insane idea pass over my lips? Once more, I did what I never wanted to. Once more, I have done what I must regret. If God existed, if any deity or spirit existed that could answer me: why must I do what I never wanted to?

I'm back to the same thing; the work of an instant. I am a despicable creature, that is the truth.

"Old bastard!" "You skunk!" "You swine!"

There's yet another one to fling these names at me. It's my successor, the big youth who calls me these names to my face. It's the voice of an outraged young man:

"Ah, the old swine!"

The broad-shouldered youth has put down his accordion. He has very thick and powerful arms. A hard pair of hands grasp me by the collar and heave me down from my spelman's seat.

"You've taken your last shit up here! Go to hell, you rotten old swine!"

I struggle and resist as much as I can, but he is a strong devil. My limbs suddenly find themselves all wobbly, without strength. My chest has grown old and constricted again. I can't breathe freely. I can offer no defense against strong, young limbs. My wretched old body is like a child's in the hands of this young man who is so big and broad all over.

I have a few tusks left in my mouth, though, four in my upper jaw, two in the lower. They are long tooth spikes, my last fangs, sharp as nails.

I sink my teeth into the hand that holds me by the collar.

"So you bite, you wretch!"

Not of my own accord will I yield to the other. If you can't protect yourself with your might, you must do it with your bite, right?

"He bites, the old son-of-a-bitch."

"Sock him one!"

"Kick his ass!"

I'm grasped by new hands. Strong young hands seize my body. Fists pummel me, feet kick me. Everywhere—punches, kicks, blows. And I lack the strength to hit back, can't manage a single punch.

"Struggle as much as you want, old son-of-a-bitch. It's all up with you!"

"Don't happen to have a stone in your pocket now, do you?"

"Now, where is that stone of yours, Anders Eriksson?"

I'm tossed in the air and fall to the ground again. Just like the girl threw my hand from hers a minute ago, I'm now thrown down from my spelman's seat in the oak.

"You've played your last tune here, old boozer. Good riddance!"

They throw my fiddle case after me. It hits me in the head. I'm banished from the spelman's throne on the hill where the oak tree stands.

I'm lying on my stomach on the ground with my head resting in hazel shrubs. I can feel the bittersweet scent of grass in my nostrils. There is a sticky, salty sensation on my tongue. Something is running from my nose reminiscent of a sudden, violent head cold. But the color of the flowing mucus is red. It's blood. I'm bleeding from the nose. They socked me a few hard ones right in my face.

And it's no wonder. I suppose all who were at the watch know it by now: Anders Eriksson was kicked down from the spelman's seat. He wouldn't give it up to the other spelman; he wanted to go on playing; and he made a total ass of himself and disgraced himself so that you never heard the likes of it: He made an improper suggestion to Gertrud and insulted her mother in the meanest way you can imagine. He has turned into a pig, the old boozer. Now, he goes after young girls at the Midsummer dance. He'll try to lure them into the bushes with him. Ever hear of such a swine! He's finished as spelman, that's for sure.

I taste blood in my mouth. The lilies of the valley under the hazel bush get blood on their leaves, it runs from me, gushes out of my nostrils, it gets thick and coagulates. I drag my hands across my nostrils and smear my entire face with it. What a peculiar, red sort of cold!

"Can I sleep with you? I slept with your mother here once."

Never did I want these words spoken. One accursed moment's work! What sort of underlying force was it that did it on my behalf? The same one that always forced me to do what I never wanted to, the one that tore apart everything good that I ever planned or wanted to accomplish in life? What will Ellen say when she hears of this? Nobody in this world has been as good to me as she. I know that nobody has wanted the best for me as she has. She knows what I am, but all she has done is try to help me with what's wrong with me. And her, I've exposed to all and sundry: I've betrayed our secret, hers and mine, the one I've been keeping and guarding as the best memory of my youth. Ellen is no young lass anymore, but an old woman, so people will laugh at her behind her back, spread it about and enlarge upon it: "Would you know, she once lay with that repulsive Anders Eriksson on the hill with the oak tree! Who would have thought she was such a hussy in her young days!"

What's most dear and precious, that is what I must needs drag through the mud! She will not be able to forgive me for it ever, will she? And never again can I bear to show myself before her.

The accursed work of one single moment has made me what I am; it has made my life hell on earth. I can't fathom what makes me do it again and again. Now, all that is left to me is regret. Now come the long days of torment. To regret—that means to swallow one's own humiliation over and over, to eat one's old spew. This, I call hell.

So I was flung down, my fiddle after me, and here I lie. I could offer no resistance, pathetic old wretch that I am. There was no stone in your pocket now, Anders Eriksson.

I should have expected this thing about the stone to have been brought up somehow. That stone I threw forty years ago. I've served time for it in jail, but it's been rolling after me all through my life. It keeps rolling after me wherever I go. It was at my heels tonight as well. I should have guessed it. That stone will follow me faithfully to the end. It will not be buried with me but will keep on rolling after I'm dead. They are tough and durable thing, stones. They keep longer than we do.

Now, you can hear a different music from the spelman's seat in the chamber of the hollow oak. It's a piece I've never heard before. It's neither a waltz nor a hambo, neither a polka nor a shottish. I can't tell what it is. But you can dance to that music as well, apparently: the dancers are circling again around the maypole at the top of the hill. Once more, the ring of dancers circle over the old human graves.

Someone else is playing now, on another instrument. It's the tone of steel and iron that penetrate my old ears. It's music without mercy I hear. I'm lying here in the hazel shrub listening to music from an instrument that has no compassion.

"Is that him lying in the bush? What happened to the old bastard?"

"Just plastered, I'd say. Sleeping his drink off."

Some other people passed by. I lie quite still, as still as a man can lie on the ground. My chest is troubling me. That rib cage where I keep my old heart has become so constricted again. It's as though my heart has swollen until there isn't enough room for it to move in there. I'm gasping for air. I can't catch my breath.

This has happened to me many times before. It will pass in a little while. But until it's over, I'll be lying here gaping like a roach thrown up on dry land.

And then, I'm so thirsty it burns my mouth and throat. Nothing to drink in either flask. There I see my own hipflask that's fallen out of my pocket. On the glass, a few red words are printed. Your health, my brother! Is my empty flask mocking me? Who was it I toasted this evening? I think it was one of my forebears, Anders Erik's Son, the one who painted my clothes chest in 1711.

The thirst is painful, smarting and making me moan. Why, but here is a spring right close by. It has running water, the clearest and purest drinking water.

I try to stand up, but I feel as if I'm suffocating. I can't get any air into my lungs. Crawling will have to do. There are only a few steps to the spring. I crawl on hands and knees. A girl's skirt, smelling of clean, newly starched cotton, sweeps close by my head. A couple is slipping away into the field vegetation bent on their own, pressing errand. They don't see the old wretch creeping along. They have other things to think about. Will the morning sun find a few red drops to shine on somewhere in the dewy grass?

At the spring, I cup my hands, and from this cup, I drink of the running water. The water is good here, transparent as sunshine and soft as a woman's lips. It quenches my thirst. With its underlying regions they say are so dark and full of all hell's dirt, how can the ground here bring forth this fresh, heavenly spring water?

I can't remember ever having been this thirsty in all my life, and I drink cup after cup. I was entirely spent as I crept here, but now, I already feel better. A minute ago, I felt removed from it all. Now, I am drinking myself back to life again. Oh, how thirsty I was! You good old spring! Our faithful old eternity spring, I'll let you rinse the blood from my face, all the blood clots out of my nose and my mouth! See how ill they have treated old spelman Anders Eriksson, faithful servant of the young and their Midsummer merriment for year after year. You know it, you spring, since you have been running through here all this time, through all the years. You've heard my fiddle and my tunes at all the vigils I've played at. You are my witness.

Spring, take my blood into your water and run off with it, so I can be clean again! Run away with it as far as you can into the north wind. You run north, don't you!

It keeps flowing and rushing, there is more and more. How strange. Won't it stop soon? A bad head cold this, the worst I ever had, this red, shivering head cold. But it doesn't matter that the blood keeps running. It will disappear in your streambed, and my face will be cleansed by your water. I hear music. There is dancing around the Midsummer pole. But someone else is playing. I shall not play here again ever.

I have quenched my thirst with your water, gentle spring. But I don't feel quite right somehow. That old trouble hasn't gone away yet. Something still feels tight in my chest. It's this unstable heart of mine that has swollen again so it doesn't have room to move inside its cage. And now, it's heaving and jumping and bursting and raising hell in there because it's run out of space. My chest feels plugged up, and that isn't so handy when you want to breathe. I'm short of breath, I need air to breathe. Spring, you've given me water to quench my thirst. Could you give me some fresh air as well, some more breath?

What's this deviltry going on in there now that prevents me from breathing? Don't know what I'll do if I can't soon . . .

But it will surely be over any minute now. I mean, it usually passes—always did before. But not a single drop of brandy do I have left to calm it with. So what can I do now? Should I start swearing or crying? Probably it won't make any difference either way. Neither crying nor swearing will fill my lungs with a breath of air.

It's my heart—and I just thought of something. When I sat playing up there a little while ago, it was my heart I was thinking of. But I can't remember what I was thinking . . . I can't remember . . . Can't remember . . .

Well, maybe I've done enough thinking. I feel it passing now. It's calming down in there, it's easing. Didn't I say so, it would go away. It will be over any moment. Only, can't remember . . .

I'm tired of it all. I'll sleep now, damn it!

Now, someone else can play.

THE SPRING

So you've returned to me, Anders Eriksson, old spelman!
Here with me, you shall remain. You have become one of
the rested.

Did you handle yourself well or poorly while in the world?
Were you a good and decent sort or brutish and evil? Were you
neither? A little of both maybe? These questions are not asked
here. Here with me, there are no questions asked and no answers
given. Here, you may hope for no restitution; there is no reward
to look forward to, neither is there any punishment to fear. I
know of no one who is evil and no one who is good. I know my
people only, and with me, all are equal. Whether my people leave
this world pleading or cursing is of no importance to me. They
come in tears, they come swearing, but come they will. You are
one of mine, Anders Eriksson, and you are back where you belong:
that is all.

You must admit that you were treated gently. You might have
been dealt a long period of suffering; you knew that many must
endure pain for a long time. But you were spared the realization
of what was happening to you. As far as you knew, you felt your

pain begin to ease and pass, and at once, you believed it was all over.

You were right, weren't you? It is all over now. Now, you have passed through. Now, you will never again be playing in this world. From now on, you will participate in the vigil of the rested. No one can boot you out from that watch—from here, no one shall ever run you off.

But now, let someone else ascend the spelman's throne and take over the playing. See, here comes a young spelman.

He is a relative of yours. He is your immediate predecessor as spelman in your family, and he was here a long time before you came. Here, you will meet all the spelmen in your family. Here with me, you will meet all your predecessors. Here, you will keep your own spelmen's vigil.

Your relative who is now approaching is much younger than you are; he is only twenty-five years old. He is dressed like no other man you met in this world. He is wearing a rough homespun jacket, very short in the back, wide breeches ending at the knees, where handsome red tassels dangle. His shirt is ruffled and shirred at the neck. On his head, he wears a tall hat with black ribbons hanging from it. Under the hat, you see his bright, yellow hair, bowl cut; you have never met anyone, relative or other, with hair such as his.

And the likes of the musical mechanism lying in his lap, you never saw. Neither did you ever hear anyone play such an instrument. You see strings stretched taut over a piece of wood that was cut from a fir tree, and in the spelman's hand, you see a bow made of horsehair.

Can you hear, as the bow glides over the strings, can you hear a fine, delicate sound? You could almost liken it to the sound of my running water flowing beneath the hill.

Listen now, Anders Eriksson, to your immediate predecessor! Hear him work his instrument as he played once upon a time, in his world, a world which is, like yours, past and left behind. Now, another sits on the spelman's throne on the oak hill: it is Anders, Erik's Son, playing his lira* on Midsummer's Night.

* See *fela,* page 10. CF. *key harp.*—Tr.

Time II

I, ANDERS, ERIK'S SON, YOUNG SPELMAN:

I pick up my music-maker and lay it on my knee. I call on my lira, and she responds to me still. I stroke my strings with the horse-hair and ask them:

"Have ye voice still?"

Their answer is clear and strong:

"We have voice still."

Last year, I sat on this hill on Midsummer's Eve, and this my lira lay in my lap and hummed singing games. She did the same the year before last year and the year before that. I am a practiced lira player, I know them well, the delicate strings that span the fret board.

Back and forth, back and forth, my hand would move the bow over them all night long as I would accompany the games and dances.

This Midsummer's Eve, I sit alone here under the oaks. The lira lies in my lap, intoning her singing games, but she must intone them for me alone.

I touch her with hands that tremble with fever. My body is cold and warm. My body shivers with cold and burns with fire. It is the wandering sickness. My throat is no longer clean. My tongue is no longer red; that is the first and sure sign. I discerned it on my tongue this morning. And I've come here tonight to seek the cure the spring can give. The water that runs here will relieve any pain and make all who are afflicted whole and sound again on St. John's Night.

Here, in this field, lie our father and mother, our sister, Katarina, in her resting place, and here is my young wife, Kerstin. I helped dig for all of them. They have all been taken by the evil sickness.

I alone remain at Högaskog. When the sun passed below the evening score at our window, I betook myself to the spring to wash and heal myself in its water.

How beauteous and bright is St. John's Night! The blossoms glow in the places where they always can be found in summer time. They send their good fragrance and sweetness to the four winds. It's the lavender that smells the strongest tonight, our church herb, our graveyard blossom. Death's smell is the strongest this Midsummer night.

I hear no birds chirping in the bushes. It's as if our songbirds have become muted and had their throats stopped up this summer. All we hear this summer is the harsh rasp from the crows sitting in endless rows on our fences along the road. They sit there hour after hour; one never sees them take flight. No one frightens the crows off—no wanderers travel our roads this year. I haven't seen a single soul since old Magda, Olov's Daughter, came from Yggersryd to fetch my little son to her home. I watched her leave through the gate, carrying my son on her back, and the crows remained where they sat on the fence pickets. One single crow actually lifted off and glided away on ponderous wings as Magda, Olov's Daughter, bore my son away.

Our farm is no longer recognizable. In our fields, where the grain would sprout green at this time, the wild grass is spreading, tall and lavish. Last year's grain, which would have sifted between my fingers into the earth by the time the oaken leaves shelter the dove, is still in the granary. Our cabbage beds lie unturned this Midsummer. There is no sound from the empty hives in our apple orchard—the swarms of bees are gone, unminded. Our cattle roam wild in the forest; only our old bell-cow can be heard lowing at the stile by evening, anxious and forlorn. All tasks have fallen behind, no longer done in their proper time. Högaskog resembles a dwelling laid waste.

It is the Midsummer festival, but no one has stuck leafy branches into the soil of our acres, no one has placed bundles of green foliage around our spring; no one has lit the fire or raised the tree at the top of the hill.

One major undertaking, however, was completed here in our acres. Many long days of toil have been spent here this spring. A significant share of our hay-making land has been dug up, all the way down to the yellow moraine.

I myself was one of the diggers, spending many weary, tiring days to prepare burial sites for our departed. These last few days, I've been alone with my shovel.

There is no one else left here in our home at Högaskog.

There were signs of foreboding as early as last summer. It began when the rye was set in ear. The weather appeared unsettled. The early summer weather was close, the air thick and stifling with pernicious mists that blocked the sun from our view. As our grain was ripe for harvesting, frost came, and snow fell on our fields. Autumn came with rain and persistent dampness. A thick, stinking fog, never seen by living men before, kept creeping up from inside the earth. It reeked, foul as a moss fire, embedded itself and stung in our nostrils, and seemed to engulf all things and lie stagnant as though it meant to stay here on earth for all times.

All through autumn, the wind blew from the south, never from the north. Our father would remark anxiously on the strange weather signs. He said it was the southerly wind that brought this tainted, harmful air all over the earth. He wished for a strong north wind.

It was by All Saints that we first heard of the wandering sickness. It was referred to by all as the battlefield sickness. It had entered our country by means of the ships returning from the lands of the East, where the war was still raging. We seldom learned anything about what went on in those regions. All we knew about King Karl was that he was with the Turks* and was remaining there. The men from our villages that had gone to war with him were not heard of again. It was assumed they had all fallen. Hitherto, we had been far removed from all cannon fire and blood and desolation. Later in the summer, however, Stenbock and other nobles had summoned troops from our country against the Danes who had entered through Skåne. That was how unrest came to settle right at our doors. Yet, the way it developed, the Jutes did not come to our land this time. Hardly had this fortuitous circumstance been made clear when it was rumored that a severe illness from the war had been brought into the country through Karlskrona.

It was not the common battlefield sickness that the ships might bring.

---

* After the defeat at Perevolotjna on July 1, 1709, Charles XII fled to the Ottoman kingdom, where he was initially welcomed by the Turks and Sultan Ahmed III and, later, because of military spending and scheming at his host's expense, put under house arrest. For five years, Charles XII sought to govern Sweden's affair while still in exile.—Tr.

Shortly before Christmas, we received grave tidings from the neighboring parish to our south; two farms in Vissefjärda had been stricken. Seamen from Karlskrona had brought it home with them. The county sheriff posted guards at the parish borders to prevent anyone from entering. They patrolled the crossroads at gunpoint, built pitch wood fires, and let no wayfarer slip by from places known to be afflicted. But rumor had it that some wagoners carrying hay to Karlskrona from the state government had been granted permission to return to their homes afterward, which later was to be much criticized.

The seasons were mixed up. The world was disoriented. We had summer heat in winter and thunder at Christmas. No one could tell the time of year from the weather outside. We all wondered at it, asking ourselves what could be causing these abnormal changes in the weather. Some were of the opinion that the sky had slipped so the earth had become dislocated and the sun had shifted out of its position. God only knew whether that was true.

Swarms of black rats appeared, bigger than any we'd ever seen in these parts before. Loathsome mice rained down from the sky; tiny, grey, scummy varmints. Each mouse had two long fangs sticking out of its mouth. As they fell, some were caught on bushes and fence pickets, where they would remain squealing for a long time. On barn walls and wood piles, we would see the mice, their mouths agape, close together like bream caught in the nets in the spawning season.

The signs awakened fear in us. Beyond doubt, a distressful year lay before us. We celebrated Christmas with solemnity. Morning and night, we said our prayers to the Lord, and every day, we burned juniper branches hoping the smoke would disinfect our house.

By Candlemas, the wandering sickness had reached our parish. Four lay dead at Källehult, two at Vackamo.

The spring heat came early. As we chopped our firewood to fill the shed for next winter, sweat drenched our clothes. None of us had seen grass so green in the month of March.

This constant southerly wind! That same, tepid south wind blew against our cheeks day in, day out. It was that wind that blew the tainted air and spread the sickness all over the earth from one place to another, said our father. He prayed to God for a harsh, severe north wind that would carry it far away from our land.

Our old father was a wise and respected man. I took over the farm after him when I married Kerstin from Yggersryd. Our father and mother remained in our care and shared in the work, and my young sister, Katarina, served in our household for her wages. With Erik, our three-year-old son, we counted six at Högaskog.

More often than not, I would follow my father's advice. Peace reigned in our home, and we were on good terms with one another. We obeyed God and the scriptures, did right by our neighbors, and cultivated our fields with care.

We had close relatives living next door. Our mother's youngest sister was married to Göran at Grönahall. The families of Grönahall and Högaskog lived in good fellowship. They'd walk down the hill to us; we'd walk up the hill to their house. Otherwise, people did not call much on one another in these worrisome times. People stopped coming to see each other, whether they were acquainted or not. We began shutting our doors to one another. Should we catch sight of a wanderer on the road that stopped to glance in the direction of our house, we'd go out into the entry and bolt the door.

The virulent fog came back in the spring to settle thickly over the earth. It stank and suffocated our mouths and nostrils. We shrank from the fog, which preceded the sickness. We cut pitch wood and built fires to drive it away. We burned juniper branches and sulfur and smudged our home and cattle barn. Our neighbors readied themselves in like fashion. Standing at the top of the hill, we could see the smoke from neighboring houses all around. The smell of burning was all over our parish this spring, from juniper, sulfur, and tar.

Next to God, nothing had more power to drive the sickness away. A sucking-calf died on us unexpectedly—a vicious sign of foreboding in addition to the others we'd seen. We buried the carcass behind the barn.

Next, our rooster became mute and stopped crowing. Our father said:

"It's best to cut the creature's head off."

He did so, but after the axe had struck, the rooster flew up onto the barn roof. There he sat flapping his wings, headless, until we poked him down from there with a pole. Father turned pale, but neither of us said a word. We had reached a time when a fowl could hover and fly about without its head.

But our farm cat went about healthy and sound, purring with well-being, sated with the plentitude of rats. Never before had there been such a wealth of rats. Our cat became fat and round as a troll.

Ere the month of March had run its course, we learned that there lay corpse upon corpse in the churchyard. Thereafter, we no longer walked up to Grönahall, and our relatives no longer came to visit us. One of us, however, would walk up to the top of the hill every day to see if smoke could still be seen from the houses of our neighbors.

We heated swine dung and breathed its steam through our noses. This became our nightly chore after we had said our prayers. We wore pouches on our chests day and night. These pouches were filled with beaver gall, camphor, and garlic. At every meal, our mother poured vinegar into our food. We also drank juniper brandy, laced with a pinch of gunpowder for half stoup.* It had a foul and bitter taste, and our sister Katarina would not drink it. We resorted to anything we believed would guard us.

But the noxious south wind still blew, and the heat weighed heavy on our limbs. My father and I became exhausted and listless as we cut firewood in the yard. Not much work was done. We told each other it would soon be time to harrow the acres.

In our house, all six of us were as yet sound. We kept to ourselves and had nothing to do with others.

But as I walked up the hill on the Day of Our Lady, I saw no smoke rise from the chimneys of Hultakvarn and Ryggamo. I returned at once to tell the rest of my household. Our father followed me back up the hill. He could see no smoke from the two neighboring farms either. Hultakvarn was farmed by a young couple that had recently moved into our parish. They had been helpful neighbors. Father and I exchanged a few words about them as we returned home.

Our father bled himself once we were back indoors. In the evening of that same Day of Our Lady, a man from the Parish Reinforcement District came pounding at our door. Father opened and stood with him outside on the doorstep. A decree had been issued forbidding any further burials in the churchyard. Whoever disobeyed the decree would be reported to the county sheriff and punished severely. From this day on, each village was ordered to establish grave sites for its own corpses out in their own grounds as convenient. The Reinforcement District had staked out a site in our close, and it was to serve the entire village. It was to be announced from the pulpit that no shrouds were to be used—bodies would simply be lowered into the earth in their clothing and buried deep.

* Archaic drinking vessel.—Tr.

That was the man's errand at our door.

Next day, Father asked me to go with him—he was heading to our close; it would do no harm to stake the place out just as a matter of course.

We crossed the meadow together. The early spring buds were opening, and the grass was up to our ankles already. The grass would be lush and plentiful when the time came for hay-making. The hill beneath the oaks was the designated place. Here, the ground was flat. Here, our young lads and lassies would play around the May trees on Midsummer's Night and build big fires. My lira would strike up dance tunes here. This was a green and lovely spot in summer time. Below ran the spring with its strengthy water.

The site lay near the parish road and could be easily reached by cart or wagon. No better spot could have been chosen in the vicinity.

We viewed the site, and our father remarked that the digging would do great damage to the hay-cutting, for the grass grew most luscious and abundant here, around the spring. I was in agreement with him; I was in agreement with father in most things. Nothing more was said about the matter, and we walked back to our house.

The very next day, we could hear the voices of those who had gone to the hill and begun digging there. We did not go over there to see which of our neighbors it might be. There was no need for any words to be exchanged between us and them—they had free access to our close. That evening, we heard the sound of a cart traveling that way.

Our mother was uneasy about not having seen any smoke out of the Grönahall chimney for two whole days. She worried about her sister and her family. Our mother was godmother to her sister's five-year-old son, and she was deeply attached to him.

To oblige our mother, I walked over to Grönahall.

I had just reached the farm and was passing through the gateway when Göran himself stepped out onto the doorstep. I recognized the black, bushy beard in his face, but his beard appeared longer and blacker than I had ever before seen it. Göran watched me approaching, his hands shielding his eyes.

I approached further and was within shouting distance. At that point, Göran called out:

"It's within the house!"

I stopped and rested my weight on my foot. Uncle Göran's voice was not to be recognized. I stood there, not knowing whether to turn around or come nearer. Göran cried once more:

"Come no further. It is in the house!"

I asked him if my aunt was still alive and if he wished to send tidings back with me. He answered that my aunt was still alive, and that he had no tidings to send back. Yet, he asked me to convey their well-wishes to all at Högaskog. He then went back inside and closed the door.

The farm nearest to ours had become contaminated. I went home and told them. Our mother asked about her nephew. He was her loveling. I had been no nearer than within shouting distance and had seen no one except for Göran himself and could thus tell her nothing about his fourth son.

At bedtime that night, Mother prayed long and earnestly to the Lord for us all. Father bled himself a second time.

The weather was still hazy and stifling; the air was thick with malignancy. It was the air that corrupted our blood, said father.

We had an anxious night. We had barely lain down upon our beds before we heard someone at our front door. I arose and went out into the entry. A wanderer stood out there, a stranger. I spoke with him through the closed door. He was a beggar come to seek shelter with us for the night. The man whimpered pitifully as he asked us to give him quarters. He had put his knapsack down on our doorstep and was leaning on his staff.

Our father called out a warning from his bed that no one would be let into our house, regardless of whether he had traveled from a known or unknown place. The beggar told us he had shunned all infected homesteads; as soon as he'd caught sight of the white cross painted on the door, he turned away and walked on. He had never been near any person in the contaminated villages. That day, he had walked through the entire parish and met no one with the exception of two gravediggers with their cart. At that encounter, he had made a long detour off the road.

Yet, our father called out:

"Do not force your way into a household that has thus far been spared. Begone!"

At that, our mother sat up in her bed and spoke more gently, saying the wandering sickness was merciless, and, therefore, we ourselves must not be unmerciful. The hardness in our hearts had brought on the sickness. Could we not let the poor wretch out there stay overnight in our barn? God would credit us our good deed.

I, too, felt pity for the poor wretch with his knapsack. This once, I felt as Mother did. Our father relented. The stranger was allowed quarter in our hay barn; I stayed several fathoms' breadth from the stranger as I showed him the way. We gave him half a stoop of skimmed milk and half a loaf of bread in the morning before he went on his way.

Come daylight, however, we noticed that the man wore a new, fine frieze overcoat over his old, tattered britches. Father watched him walk away and wondered where he had gotten that overcoat. Finding clothes to shield one's body was an easy task in these times. So many bodies were buried in the earth, and there were clothes left from all the deceased. Father claimed he had seen the beggar's new coat before. Then, it had been worn by the young farmer at Hultakvarn. Were that to be true, it would be a peculiar thing indeed. It would mean that the man had been lying when he insisted he had passed all the homesteads by where the sickness had struck.

The week of Easter had arrived. As late as Palm Sunday morning, we found ourselves as yet all well at Högaskog. We prepared for our Easter celebration with thankfulness that we had so far been spared.

By Palm Sunday evening, my young sister Katarina began complaining. She felt shivers without as she was burning up within. We told her to show her tongue. She did so, and we knew—her tongue was black as the coal in the mine.

The first day and night, she lay as though in a deep sleep. No one touched her except for Mother, who gave her what to drink. The second day, the blue-black buboes began swelling up all over her body. They swelled up like rising dough in her groins and armpits. Her head throbbed with pain; she felt unquenchable thirst and was deeply terrified.

Mother mixed crushed red onion, honey, sweet milk, and some of my sister's urine and boiled it into a porridge, which she wrapped inside a linen cloth and placed around Katarina's neck and chest. The poultice was to open the pustules so the pus could seep out.

From what we could observe, the poultice was of little help to her. Our mother tried other remedies. My sister suffered such pain and lay shrieking for hours on end upon her bed, moaning till her voice gave out.

There was yet one remedy known to help against the sickness. Our father mentioned it: When a maiden had her blossoms for the first time, she was to collect them in a clean linen cloth and lay them to dry in the sun. Once dry, the cloth was to be kept and guarded carefully, for if the linen cloth that contained the maiden's roses were to be steeped in vinegar and wrapped around the buboes at the time of sickness, it would draw the poison out. No one knew of a place where such a remedy could be obtained, however. It was no longer the custom for a young maiden to collect her first roses and keep them safeguarded.

On Wednesday morning of Holy Week, Katarina lay silent on her bed. Her complexion had altered, and she was no longer recognizable. Her breath stank, her face was blotchy, and her eyes were narrow slits within the seething black dough of her cheek buboes. This was the third day, and we were preparing ourselves to see blood well from her nose and mouth.

Father said we might as well head up to the meadow with a shovel each.

By now, several of our neighbors lay buried at the chosen site. We found one shovel, left behind under a hazel bush. We dug deep, father and I. We dug down to the clay; father said that was deep enough.

In the evening of Wednesday in Holy Week, our sister Katarina expired. Our father washed all dirt from our old stone cart; we placed her in the cart, still wearing the clothes she had been lying in, and carried her away to the close. Our sister was slight of build and not heavy to pull. Our mother went with us, and at the open grave, we sang a psalm: life on earth shall reach its end; Heaven brings eternal life. When we had thrown the dirt back into her grave, we placed our shovels in the hazel bush along with the one already waiting there.

On our way home, we encountered Göran at Grönahall. He was pulling a hay drag behind him, one we had often seen him use on the marshy meadows. A skin rug covered the drag, and under the rug lay his wife, our mother's youngest sister. Mother asked about her godson, the five-year-old, and learned that he was still alive and sound.

Only now, through Göran, did we learn that Yggersryd, the child-hood home of my wife, Kerstin, had been struck this week. It was not known to him if any of its inhabitants had been buried, how-ever. We asked about Hultakvarn and Ryggamo. Göran said: "They have been there from the Reinforcement District. The houses have been closed down."

Thus, I was forced to tell Kerstin that the sickness had reached her childhood home.

On Maundy Thursday, we slaughtered our winter ram in prepa-ration for Easter. As we stood around the slaughtering block, the sun was baking down on the barn wall as though it were the middle of summer. An evil stench hovered over the earth, and it plagued us in the heat.

On Easter Saturday, our father dropped as he was watering the animals in the barnyard. He lay there, calling to us that he did not wish to be carried into the house. He crawled into the barn and lay down in what remained of the hay we had been using as winter fodder. The unknown beggar had made his bed there when he had come seeking quarter with us for the night. Our father was con-vinced that this man had brought the sickness to our home. He had carried it with him in the new frieze overcoat he had stolen at Hultakvarn. This was what our act of mercy gained us. What was done was done, however.

Our mother would not regret a good deed. She trusted that God would count it in our favor when we arose from the dead on judgment day. We were all destined to die when God so willed it; so if death did not come by means of the beggar's overcoat, the Lord might send it in a thousand other ways.

Our father lay in the barn with a jug of water beside him. His body shivering. During the day, he uttered not a sound, but at night, I heard him moan. He forbade us all to cross the barn threshold. We stood in the doorway and spoke with him. He told us what to do with his remains when it was all over: all his life, he had obeyed the authorities, but now, there was one decree from the county sheriff that he refused to comply with: He would not be buried in his dirty work clothes. With him he wanted his pristine bridal sheet that had been kept in the wooden chest along with Mother's all through the years since their wedding and which he had intended as his burial clothes. We must swear by our eternal bliss to remove his work clothes, which we could burn if we wished to. Furthermore, I was to cover him well. He spelled out what field I was to use to plant the barley next spring, and other such things.

On the morning of Easter Sunday, he called to me: he felt I might as well go and start digging his grave. I went to the meadow and began digging. I kept digging all through Easter Sunday for Father. The weather was stifling, breathing was difficult. I became thirsty and drank from the flowing spring. By evening, Father was near death, his speech delirious. He was dividing his belongings between Katarina and me, forgetting that my sister no longer walked among the living.

By Easter Monday, it was over. We took his bridegroom sheet out of the clothes chest and wrapped him in it as he had told us, and we burned his work clothes. I pulled the cart. Mother and my wife, Kerstin, walked behind and helped push it up the hill. Our father had been a heavy man, tall and strong of build. Now, the grasses stood thick in the meadow, the anemones were fully opened, and the cowslip buds were near bursting. I covered Father with great care as he had instructed me. He had heard rumors of carrion eaters digging up the graves and feasting upon the corpses. At the end, we read a psalm and said the Lord's Prayer.

Eight days later, I lowered our mother in the ground. I alone pulled the cart that time. There was no need for Kerstin to push from behind. Mother was not heavy.

That night, I lay awake for a long time before sleep came. The graveyard in our close was not consecrated ground, and Mother had fretted over the eternal salvation of her soul. It had been whispered that in the night, people had buried their dead in the churchyard. It was done without pastor or pastor's knowledge. But we at Högaskog were afraid to go against the stern decree. I had placed our mother in unsacred ground, even though she had longed so desperately for the comfort of the churchyard. Sleep did not come easily. Could this decree from the Parish Reinforcement District mean that our mother would suffer in hell for all eternity? I felt that those who had denied her the churchyard would have to vouch for her before God. I was finally comforted by that thought.

Three living souls—my wife, my son, and I—still remained at Högaskog.

We were now in the month of May, and the stifling weather continued. All the signs of spring were backward. No cuckoo sang from the treetop. No songbirds sat trilling on their branches as they would normally do from morning till night; but crows and ravens could be seen flying about in droves and sitting close together in big, huddled-up clusters on the roofs of the houses. We could smell fox fur near the walls of our houses. Our house cat became even fatter and was now so rotund that he rolled along rather than walked. It was a blessed time for animals of his kind. We began to wonder if the predators would be the only living beings left in this world.

I bled my wife and myself. We burned our used bedclothes and smudged our house with pitch wood. But a foul, sweetish odor clung to the walls and the floor. We sensed the sickness lying in readiness in nooks and crannies. We were careful with food and drink. We ate just enough to keep life within our bodies and drank no unboiled liquid.

Draught had set in, and our well was beginning to dry out. In brooks and rivulets, mire was showing in shallow places, and foul odors rose from the bottom. From dried-out hollows rose the stench of death, of fish gone sour. In the lake, stone protruded from the surface, stones we had never before seen above water.

And yet, up in the meadow, our old spring ran in its flow as always, cold and clear. My wife said that if we were spared until Midsummer, we would survive: On St. John's Night, the spring water would once more regain its power, and we could make use of it. Then, the spring would keep us safe from the fearful sickness.

But my wife, Kerstin, was to be the fourth one to sicken at Högaskog.

It took seven days and nights for her. The last days, she lay as though asleep. Her face retained its clear, delicate hue until the very last day. Then, her face altered. She spoke of our son and said:

"Comfort him! Comfort our Erik."

Our father and mother had been old. Katarina and Kerstin had must lay down their young lives. Kerstin was eighteen when we married. She had twenty-two years of life.

Digging for her was more exhausting then for any of the others. Once and again, I needed to sit down and rest. The soil lay so heavy in my shovel, and my limbs felt tired and leaden. It was fortunate that the weather had cooled off some, and the fetid south wind had ceased blowing at last. Still, digging was done at a snail's pace. I had become slow-moving.

Our bridal sheets lay folded away in the chest since our wedding. They were to be used one more time only, and for one of us, that time had already come. I unfolded the sheet that was Kerstin's and wrapped it around her. The birches were in foliage, and I dressed our stone cart with branches. Then, I made sure Erik was safely inside the house before I headed off. But he climbed up onto the window ledge and kept staring after me as I left the house with the cart. He showed good sense for his years.

Kerstin seemed heavier to pull than my father, mother, or sister. Perhaps that was in my imaginings only, since I had become so listless and sluggish of limb.

In the meadow, most of the flowers were in full bloom. I cut a few pieces of turf with lots of blossoms on them and lay them over Kerstin with the green side up. No one else within this grave site had been covered with flowering turf before their graves were closed.

I found my son still standing there, staring out through the window as I returned home with the empty cart. He asked why his mother had been riding in it this time rather than walking behind to push it, as she had done before. Several times through the day, he asked me what I had done with his mother. Erik was keen-witted though he was only three.

Now, there were only the two of us left among the mortals at Högaskog. The days dragged.

In our clothes chest, one bridal sheet lay waiting. I could not refrain from thinking about that. I thought of myself. So, the next morning, I went to the close and started digging again. I dug right close to Kerstin.

I could work for a few hours only. I returned the following day and dug further. But I was slow.

Another resting place had been finished. The task was now old and familiar, and I felt as if I had stood here on the hill and dug all my life. Yet, I had an inkling that this time would be the last.

As I woke in the morning, I told my little son to show me his tongue. I saw it was healthy and red. Then, I stretched my own tongue out and showed it to Erik, and he told me it was red.

Saying my morning prayer, I thanked God. Then, I went out and milked the bell-cow who would still return from pasture at night. I made us barley porridge and hot milk. All day, I kept the fire burning in the stove, so that the smoke would show that there were still folks alive at Högaskog.

It was lonely to hear no other treads over the floorboards than Erik's and mine. I began dreading our silent house. I worried over Erik, who might be left all alone after me. I thought about whether or not to shut the house up and move us out into the forest and build us a brush hut.

Every morning, we inspected each other's tongues.

The days were long. I went about in sad bereavement. Soon, I recognized nothing in this desolate world. No wanderer came along the road. On the fences, the crows sat unmoving. I heard nothing of friends and relatives. From Kerstin's childhood home at Yggersryd, we had heard nothing since spring. Before Kerstin died, it had been rumored that someone remained alive in the house.

One Monday in May, I had taken to collecting one wood chip each week, and now, we had reached the fourth week. June had arrived. Midsummer would be here soon.

I had begun to wonder if anyone was left in the neighboring homesteads. I worried more and more about my little son, who might be left alone. One day, I shut Erik inside the house and left to roam through the neighborhood and look for people.

It was eerily quiet on the road. I met no one. No one stirred in the fields and meadows. I did see some animals. A horse gone wild was grazing in a rye field, and a couple of cats were fighting over some carrion by the roadside, and I glimpsed the tail of a fox slinking away into the bushes. At the top of the hill, I halted. No smoke could be seen in the immediate neighborhood. Further off, I could see smoke rising from three homesteads, but I would have to walk quite far through the parish to reach them.

I walked to the neighboring farms. At Ryggamo, not a living thing stirred outside the house. I saw the white cross painted on the door, then I turned away.

I walked on to Hultakvarn. The buildings lay empty and closed up. A sweetish odor filled the air. It appeared that someone lay unburied inside the house. Outside the dwelling-house, a large quantity of bed straw had been spread; there lay a heap of skin rugs, and on the doorstep I found a pot that held porridge covered with fuzzy, green mould. No jaw would ever again be chewing food in this house.

Thus, I wandered through the desolate countryside. The people had vanished. Their belongings lay abandoned. Yet, over the misery, the sun shone, and the ground was clad in green. This was the saddest woe this land had suffered ever.

As I reached Grönahall, however, the home of our relatives, I could see from afar that something was afoot among the buildings. As I came closer, I saw that it was a small child who was loitering by the cellar airhole. The child wore a long, black coat that reached to the ground, and its matted hair hung down over the collar. It was not possible to judge from the clothes whether it was a boy or a girl. I surmised it was a boy, since Göran of Grönahall had not had a daughter of a comparable age. The child over there had to be our mother's godson and loveling, the youngest son of Grönahall.

The little boy stood holding a stick and was poking around in a pile of turnips outside the cellar. As soon as he caught sight of me, he threw the stick away from him and ran toward the grain fields.

The child was terrified of people. I halted and called to him: "Do not be afraid. It is Anders of Högaskog."

The boy had run to a mound of stones right in the middle of the cornfield. There, he stopped and stared at me. I called to the little one in a friendly tone and walked out into the field. Then, he suddenly crept inside the mound of stones. When I arrived, he had disappeared among them.

It became clear to me that the abandoned child at Grönahall would go into hiding within the mound of stones as soon as anyone came near the farm. I noticed a hollow between two large stones. That had been his entry. It was large enough for a child, and too small for a grown man. I could not follow him.

I stayed by the mound of stones, waiting. Now and then, I'd call: "Come out! There is nothing to fear."

Once, I thought I heard a sound from the pile of stones, a sound resembling a sob; but the child did not return.

I walked over to the buildings and waited there, watching the mound of stones in the field carefully. Perhaps the boy would venture forth again once he believed the visitor had gone his way. But any movement would have been thoroughly concealed by the stones. No one came forth.

One corner in the barn where the fodder was kept revealed the indentation from a small body. Here was where the little one had found his bed at night.

I returned home to Högaskog but could not forget the child who had crept in among the stones and not come out again.

The following day, I went again to Grönahall. This time, I could discern no life near the buildings. I went to inspect the fodder barn, but the hollow in the hay did not appear to have been used since the previous day. I looked in every hidey-hole around the homestead but could not find a single trace of its youngest dweller. I found a few wooden trundles, carved from an alder log, as well as a small poker, made for a child. Here, he had struck at the wood, he had played alone, even though it took at least two to play the game.* In the

* *Trundle*—a circular wheel-shaped piece of wood, 6 inches in diameter, thrown between two opponents. The thrower would use enough force to try and land the trundle past the goal line of the opposing party. The

days when I took part in these youthful games, I would gladly strike the wood; I would drive my opponent back with strong thrusts.

All seemed to indicate that the abandoned child was still inside the mound of stones. I called out into the opening between the stones with as much voice as I could muster:

"Step out, little one! If you'll just come out, you and I shall throw the trundle."

There was no answer. Then, I decided to force my way into the mound of stones. I heaved away the stones I was able to shift. They were not many. Soon, I was hindered by the size of the stones, well anchored in the soil, and they simply would not budge. I could not move them one inch, try as I might. I would never be able to reach farther into the mound single-handed. It would require the strength of at least three full-grown men to move the earthbound stones and gain entry.

For a single man, there was nothing more to be done.

Yet, I could not forget the abandoned child at Grönahall. The next day, I went to that homestead for the third time. This time, a pair of large cats run wild were loitering near the mound of stones in the field. They sat, fat and contented, indolently licking their lips. I threw stones at the wild cats and tried to run them off. They angrily showed their teeth and hissed at me. Then, they slunk away through the hole where the child had disappeared three days ago.

I tried shifting the large stones once more but was forced to abandon my efforts. I could do nothing here. I walked around all the buildings of the farm, searching. I did not want to abandon all hope, but I found not a trace of the little one.

---

opponent would attempt to stop the momentum of the trundle with pokers and, if successful, would force the other party to withdraw to the line where the trundle landed. Primarily played on the roads.—Tr.

Thus, I never was able to find him, the last living being at Grönahall; he was of our family, and his fate presaged to me what might happen to my own son. Day and night, I could think of nothing else. I made my decision. I would walk to Yggersryd to see if anyone was still alive in Kerstin's childhood home.

Yggersryd was a lone homestead out in the woods, a long walk off. No sooner had I turned into the gateway than I saw a figure seated on the doorstep. It was an old woman wearing a red cap on her head. She was screening last year's peas into a bowl. Her form was shrunken and small, but she looked up at me with clear, steady eyes: It was Magda, Olov's Daughter, my wife's grandmother.

"Are you the only one left at Yggersryd?"

"There is no one else left. I mind the farm."

There sat the old woman in her red cap, like a small house gnome on her doorstep. Magda, Olov's Daughter, alone remained in good health in a house where the rest of its dwellers had succumbed to the illness. She had lived more years than any of the ones gone before her.

"You have come for help, Anders?"

"Should I be taken, my little son will be left alone."

"I can walk back with you and take him home with me. Magda, Olov's Daughter, will be spared."

God had ordained that her life would be spared, that was a fact we could place our trust in. It was God's intent that someone should remain to guard the dwelling at Yggersryd.

Magda, Olov's Daughter, accompanied me back to Högaskog, walking on legs no less swift than mine. When she again left my home, she carried our little Erik on her back.

I stood outside the house, watching the old woman carry my son off. She passed through the gate and turned up the hill. On both sides of the road, the fearless crows sat on the fences. One crow alone lifted sluggishly and flew on heavy wings up toward the meadow. Magda, Olov's Daughter, kept her arms around the little one's legs, and he wound his arms around her neck. From a distance, he appeared like a hump on the old woman's shoulders. My son's head was turned away from me. I could no longer see his face.

Magda, Olov's Daughter, vanished behind a large hazel bush by the roadside, carrying on her back what would be my family's whole life if I were gone.

I was alone at Högaskog. The days grew even longer. There still remained a few days until Midsummer.

No one traveled the roads. The crows sat undisturbed on their pickets. The world was without songbirds.

I kept the fire going in the stove and baked my bread on the coals. I kept to the house and sought no one in the neighborhood anymore. Once, I walked to the spot in the meadow. I could already see green growth sprouting on the upturned sods. It did not appear as though any one had come here to dig after me. I had finished my digging near Kerstin.

Awakening on the morning of Midsummer's Eve, however, I felt a new, unfamiliar sensation in my body. I did what I had done every morning: I stretched out my tongue to see. Yet, I knew what was happening before I saw my outstretched tongue. My body had told me:

My tongue was no longer red.

I awaited St. John's Night. When the setting sun reached the evening score of the window post, I went to the spring that takes away all suffering.

I had my place here last year as well as the two years before. Here, on this hill under the oak trees, is the spelman's time-honored place. It is the Midsummer feast, and I brought my music-making gear with me. Thus, a young spelman is once again seated here as in years gone by.

I, Anders, Erik's Son, sit here playing my lira on Midsummer's Night.

The same way one would grasp one's sweetheart round her waist to set her on one's knee, so have I placed my music-maker on my knee. Oh, my lira, I was just a little fellow the day I divined your riddle, as told by the old folks:

"I am wood from the fir, sheep's gut and mare's hair, I was raised in the forest, dressed in the sheep's pen and bred in the stable, and now, I lie in your lap playing singing games." Thus reads the riddle of the lira.

Your spelman's tongue has blackened. But yours, my lira, is fresh and red, and this night, you sing out of your sound bosom:

"Sweet it is to live; cruel it is to die."

But, come sunrise, I will drink myself hale from our spring here. From her veins flows health. Into the deep earth, the dead are lain. From within the deep earth, life springs forth. Thus read the riddle of life and death.

Here, I shall seek my cure. Yet, no one has placed branches around the meadow spring this year. Last year, leafy, green branches adorned the spring all around. We wound green leaves around our hats and turned ourselves out right handsomely. We elected the Midsummer bride and built the big fire here upon the hill. Kerstin and I were the last couple to have celebrated our wedding, and we were allowed to light the fire. And the young lads and lasses played their games and danced here all through St. John's night, jumped across the fire with both feet together, struck the third, ran the widow's game, vaulted over the pole, turned the hare skin inside out, picked flowers from under the snow drift, and played hundreds of pranks.

The year that Kerstin of Yggersryd turned seventeen, we elected her as our Midsummer bride. All in merry jest, we dressed her in bridal clothes, placed a floral wreath on her head and a silver chain around her neck. A fairer Midsummer bride there never was. Kerstin was glad of the honor and yet saddened and downcast, for the saying goes:

"The lass who's a bride at the Midsummer feast shall never be wed to her bridegroom by priest."

I had my lira with me, and we all sang and trolled in the dances and games. I twirled the Midsummer bride around, and, she and I, each in turn, we sang the lines of the singing game. We sang "The suitor and the lass." Kerstin sang the lass's questions:

"Whose bread shall I bake? Whose bed shall I make? Whose child shall I carry? Whose arms shall I sleep in at night?"

And, as my turn came around in the song, I gave her the answers of the suitor:

"My bread shall you bake! My bed shall you make! My child shall you carry! My arms shall you sleep in at night!"

There were more lines to the song, but they were so mournful that they did not suit the gladsome mood of the youthful games, thus were seldom sung.

Kerstin said:

"You are dancing with one who shall never marry."

"You shall marry me," I replied.

"Shall I," she asked, "When? When the lame dance? When the raven learns to sing? When there are seven Thursdays to the week?"

"It will not be as long as that," I said. "In one year's time, I shall be of age."

She grew silent for a moment, then, before she answered me: "If you have not forgotten me by next Midsummer, ask me again to marry you!"

Such was the jocular preamble to what came to grow between Kerstin and me at the Midsummer watch when she was the chosen Midsummer bride.

Once the clamorous games had been played, it was time for the silent watch—two by two, one lad and one lass to themselves, until the sun rose. Kerstin and I were a pair; we kept the silent watch together. And before we parted on the morning of Midsummer's Day, she had in truth been my bride—there had been no make-believe. We embraced and bedded each other on the ground. A girl who had served as Midsummer bride would not be held accountable for it afterward. She remained as honorable still, considered as truly a maiden afterward as much as before. The priest had tried to prohibit our yearly dressing of a Midsummer bride; he had met with no compliance anywhere. The strictures of chastity did not apply on Midsummer's Night. All we had done was play as young lads and lasses had always played during the shortest night of the year.

Kerstin was so moved while we held each other. Later, she went and washed in the running waters of the spring. I knew why she had done so, but I wanted to test her.

"Do you think the water will help you?"

"They say it has helped girls before me," she said.

"You know what the old folks call the spring," I said.

"I would say I know it well."

She had removed her stockings, which she held in her hand while she dipped her bare feet into the runnel of the spring. In the clear water, her toes shone like tiny pebbles. The spring coursed and purled between them. The sun had just risen with one ray slicing down into the watercourse like the edge of a scythe.

Kerstin had been sitting by the spring with her face turned away. Now, she turned to me and said:

"Look away, will you?"

I obeyed, somewhat sheepishly. For a little while yet, I heard her splattering in the runnel; she was still at her errand to the spring at sunrise.

Then, she came back to me, barefoot as before; she stepped cautiously through the grass, her stockings dangling from her hand. Her cheeks were still rosy.

She smiled at me and said:

"Now, I am a maiden once more."

"Did you say the right spell?" I asked.

"I read it to the spring," she said.

"Read it to me as well!"

"I reckon there would be no harm in that," she said.

So, Kerstin sat down in the dewy grass and read me the spell of the spring:

"Little maid, come here!
Did he hurt you, dear?
Swift and sure is
My clear water, here, the cure is
If he hurt you, dear.
Little maid, come here!"

So read the girls who went to the meadow spring on the morning of Midsummer's Day. So read Kerstin to me; meanwhile, her face was turned from me.

A blessed spring it was that coursed through the meadow, a spring with the power of healing. She took from us all hurt that we brought to her, carried it away with her in her runnel; and that was because this spring ran north. And she helped the girls and wiped out all traces of the Midsummer night nuptials. They cleansed themselves in her running water, which made them chaste and respectable once more. The spring gave them back their maidenheads.

The old people called her "the brides' spring." And what recourse would a Midsummer bride have had without the spring in the meadow?

On the tip of each blade of grass, a dewdrop was glistening. I filled my cupped hands with the dew from the grass and leaves and touched Kerstin's forehead with it. I said:

"No pain and no wounds shall be brought within this year to thee."

She in turn collected dew from the grass and touched it to my forehead. Both of us had thus been guarded against all sickness for that year.

Consequently, we celebrated our wedding, Kerstin and I. It was the first one in our close, the second one in her childhood home at Yggersryd. Our own first wedding, however, remained our own secret, never to be shared except by the two of us.

A year went by before Kerstin was to lie in my arms again. That happened the following summer as she became a bride for all to behold. At our first wedding, we had no other witnesses than the coursing spring. At our second one, the priest, the precentor, and all our neighbors were present, and the bride wore the silver wreath belonging to the church. We had the spring to thank for her right to wear that wreath. On the eve of our wedding, we went up the hill in the meadow and lowered our gratitude into the deep water: a whole silver daler.*

* Used throughout Europe during the eighteenth century, based on a given silver content. CF. *thaler.*—Tr.

Accordingly, Kerstin placed the wifely kerchief on her head and moved to our home at Högaskog. She kneaded her first bread dough and set it to rise over Midsummer dew. This was one summer of our lives as any other summer with the budding in May, the June flowering, the ripening in July, and the cutting and harvesting in August. My young wife and I gloried in our good days. We gloried in our nights even more.

Kerstin was well contented in my arms, and I in hers. The things she whispered in my ears in bed, I treasured in my heart and will always treasure. Every part of her, every one of her limbs, her body and her soul, all vouched for her telling me what was true. Her womb that so willingly opened for my hand spoke for her. The sweet lips of a woman may lie; her womb cannot. A woman's hands may lie as they caress you, but the womb she offered to me could not. Not one false caress had I from Kerstin. Like the sound of the smallest songbird came her whisper when she was with me and I was inside her:

"Anders, my lira man and felekarl!* Could God in his greatness have anything lovelier in store for us up in that heaven of his? So, I wish I might keep you near me always until our days are at an end. Say, do you not wish it so also, Anders, my felekarl?"

She was proud of me when I was complimented on my playing of the lira. She was otherwise shy in the presence of strangers, but at such times, she'd gently touch my ear with her hand. Anders felekarl, that was what she called me. Kerstin Midsummer bride, that is what I called her. Well, that would embarrass her and bring fire to her cheeks. I remember how red they glowed the time when she was a bride with neither precentor nor priest.

---

* *Felekarl,* "fiddlefellow," see *fela,* page 10. *Karl* from Old English *carl,* from Old Norse *karl,* man, carl—a man of the common people.—Tr.

The crops were splendid that year. We cut much hay in the meadow. We mowed and raked for many a long, hot day. We amassed the haycocks until the shadows grew long on the ground at night and the wind blew cool under the trees. We cocked the hay until sunset. We could be satisfied with our day's work, said our father. He tired more quickly than we, who were young. Our father went home, but Kerstin and I kept working. Before returning to our house that evening, we embraced in the windrow of cut hay. We could get our fill neither by day nor by night.

Then, one day in August, Kerstin confided in me while we were sheafing the leafy birch twigs in the close: the next generation of our family had made himself known. If all went well and ran according to its timely course, we would be able to have a christening feast ere spring arrived.

By winter, Kerstin's breasts became heavy and distended; she walked more slowly and trod more heavily over the floorboards.

My bed shall you make! My child shall you carry!

The game "The Suitor and the Lass" was nearing its close.

In bed at night, Kerstin would grasp my hand and say:

"Feel how he digs his heels in, the new one at Högaskog!"

I placed my hand there and was glad to feel the strength of this being that was kicking inside its mother's womb. It was already stirring in there, the next generation. The children have always been the greatest riches of all families, and I was next in line to acquire these riches. Here, I felt a beginning had been made, and it was promising.

So the sun travels its course for a pregnant woman through the nine signs, and the moon rises nine times anew. If the bridal bed is made by summer solstice, the childbed will be readied by the vernal equinox. That can be easily determined. And all went well and all happened in its proper time. When the sallow bush bloomed, our

son was born. He was christened Erik after our father. He thrived
quickly and grew from his mother's milk.

Our old father needed some relief from all his toils, and I grew
more preoccupied with the running of the farm. The daily chores
and worries made me exhausted at night. I forgot my music and
seldom had time to pick up my lira. But Kerstin said:

"Remember that you are Anders felekarl!"

And some cool summer evening or other, I might sit down on
the front step with my lira in my lap. Our son was already beginning to stand up on his legs, and he followed me around wherever
I went. I sat outside our house and played for my son.

Around the house, the fields lay silent and ripening at dusk. At
such times, I might start wondering about one recurring riddle:

I'd see our father walk toward his bed at night ever more slowly,
and I observed our son move ever more swiftly around me. I noticed
the slowing steps of one and the quickening steps of the other.
The old body was receding; the young body was springing forth.
Our father, old Erik, Anders' son, would leave us, but Erik, my
son, had come in his stead: Erik, Anders' Son, passed away—and
still remained.

Such was the course of generations on this earth. They passed
on, and yet, they stayed.

I mowed the grass that grew in the meadow last year, but this
year, it has all grown back. I mowed it again. It was wetted by the
same rain, was dried by the same sun, and I harvested it anew.
Still, next year, it would grow back. The grass always grew in the
meadow, no matter how often I cut and harvested it.

Was our family not like the grass that grew in our close? It grew,
fell, was raked and gathered as hay, but every year, at its set time,
it would grow back green in its place.

From the leftover roots of last year's grass, new blades grew; from
a man's member, new shoots would spring. From our father's seed,

I had sprung, and from mine, our son was growing, yet, my seed stemmed from our father, all three in our family had the same seed. Were we not all the same man, who was bred, born, died, and was buried, to be bred, born to live again?

And I looked to the coming years that awaited us, I could imagine a hundred summers of growing and flowering meadow grass, I could picture my grandson's grandson walking across the field, the scythe in his hand. He would still carry the seed within him from all of us here at Högaskog.

Thus, I'd sit on our doorstep in the summer evenings, reflecting on the passing and rebirth of the generations. In my lap, my lira lay, humming singing games to my son—he who was the tender shoot, he who would carry our family's continued existence after me.

That was last year and the year before that. This year, I am the only one left at Högaskog.

I tremble with the shivers; I burn with fever. My tongue is black. My body is bulging with my corrupted blood. Who shall still my shivers? Who shall cool my fever? Who will make my tongue red once more? Who will cure my buboes? Who will cleanse my poisoned blood? Who will make me hale and fit?

The spring will. The spring here will give me the cure. The spring will take the evil from me and carry it away with her in her runnel. When the sun rises, I will be well again. Anders, Erik's Son, shall remain among the living. For a long time yet shall I wander with my scythe across the meadow.

Up here is where we lay in the arms of one another, Kerstin and I, when she was Midsummer bride. Here, the ground received the blood she gave for the benefit of the next generation. Here, she visited the brides' spring, and then, she returned and said:

"Now, I am a maiden once more."

Kerstin and I were so young in this world, just at the outset of our lives together. We could have lived happily as man and wife for a long time. Our lot on this earth is part of the riddle of the generations that no one can solve. God has placed this riddle before us. No one has as yet guessed its answer.

We never sang that song to the end that time, Kerstin and I. The second part of the game was not sung; we left it out. We decided it could wait. But we have reached the point where the game will have to be sung to its end. The lass asks her questions, the suitor gives his answers, and the game runs through its last verses:

"Whose linen shall I wind? Whose child shall I soothe? Whose death shall I mourn? Whose arms shall I sleep in at night?"

"My linen shall you wind. My child shall you soothe. My death shall you mourn. My arms shall you sleep in at night."

THE SPRING

Welcome, Anders, Erik's son!

So, you have come to me with your soot-black tongue, your stifled bosom, your festering buboes, your infected body. There, in my waters, you sought the cure. You trusted in me; and I did not fail you. I fail no one who is one of mine. I am your source of remedy and the only one you can safely rely upon. From me, you will receive the sole cure available to you: You will be granted your return!

In mortal fear, you reached your tongue out to inspect it every morning. You suffered great anxiety. Still, I never troubled or felt anxious over you. Why should I? All the time, you were in the utmost safety—you belonged to me, and your return was assured.

Welcome! I greet you!

You have fulfilled what was required of you. You have ensured the next branch of your family tree. Your own life, you shall renounce for the sake of life itself.

Here, you will stay among the flowers and the grasses. Over you, the scythes will cut and the rakes will swing. Young, hurried feet will walk over you in the hay windrows, when the evening has cooled off in the meadow. Swift and blushing, someone approaches. Quietly, still blushing, someone walks away. The flow of years will course over the earth—the oaks will thicken and grow older—but no one counts the years that pass.

Here, you will remain as long as the grass keeps growing and the flower keeps opening up her calyx; as long as the sun keeps shining and the rain gives moisture; as long as the wind yet sweeps by and bends the blade on the ground; as long as I find my outlet here at the foot of this hill while I follow the lives of generations coming and going.

The scythe will cut, the rake will gather, but you shall neither take pleasure in the good harvest, nor shall you fret over failed crops. You shall feel no joy over anything gained. You shall feel no sorrow over anything lost. You will not quicken with the sun, not stiffen with the frost. You shall take no pleasure in good health, and sickness will leave you untroubled. You shall neither rejoice at life, nor fear death. You are with me, your healing spring, who takes all hurt away.

Nevermore shall you know anxiety. You are not part of the large tribe that lives on the outside. Your bed is calm, your bedfellow is peace; lighter than bird's down will be your cover.

Here, you shall remain for a long time.

Here, it will go on, our game and our vigil. Here, they will all gather, the spelmen of your blood. The third one will now have his turn.

The fiddle has sounded, the lira has sung from your knee. The time has come for another voice—we shall now hear from the piper of your ancestry.

So, step forth, you who have skill with the side-blown flute!* Step out of the depths of your century, so greedy for life! Step forth and play! It is time for you to relieve the others for a while. You are

---

* Also "transverse flute."—Tr.

the one who will now ascend the spelman's throne on the hill under the oak trees.

Listen! Hear him sound his pipe at present. Hear! It is Anders, the piper, playing Midsummer's Night.

For the oak trees, this is the time of their youth.

Time III

I, Piper Anders:

Thus, I find myself the only one left here on the hill. It is the bright time of night. God's pipes are sounding from bush and branch. I pull out my own pipe to join in their playing.

Blossoms glow around me in the meadow. Here shines thyme with its red crown; here floats the scent of spearmint and the blue lavender. Here, one can gather lad's love, sage, hyssop, and lemon balm, and this completes the bunch of our church's seven holy herbs. Seven are the mortal sins, and seven are the holy herbs to be picked during the Sabbath and proffered within God's house. Each wretch must pick one herb for each sin that would otherwise bring him death.

Yet, for each of the sins I have committed, I should by rights offer two. When the sun rises, which she will do presently, she could never shine on a worse sinner than Piper Anders.

What is it that I have done since the sun last rose? I have caroused and wagered; I have played and frolicked, led others in wanton dancing, and I have whored most infamously. I have committed the sin of lust, one of the seven that will bring on death. Lust is the sin that most besets me, says Master Lambert, our parish priest.

It will soon be over, this night of capital sin, and through my head roars the mighty surge of penitence. I shall be brought to book and be questioned:

"How have you comported yourself within the sun circle of this day and night, Piper Anders?"

I understood it suddenly, sitting here under the young oak tree— I am bound for hell.

On the morn of Midsummer's Eve, I awoke with the daylight on the cot in my solitary hut and was thirsty. Roughly, I tore the tap from the ale keg, but not a single drop ran out of it. I turned the keg over; it was dry as a piece of newly burned woodland. I grew dejected and short of temper and kicked it with my foot so a slat flew out of it. I seized the jug standing by the hearth and walked to the spring in the meadow to fetch water.

The weather for our Midsummer feast promised to be glorious. A pair of playful squirrels kept chasing one another among the hazel bushes. I halted and looked for fruit in the thicket of hazel. Since it had rained on St. Urban's Day,* there would be no rot in the nuts this year. I made my mind up to collect a few bushels' worth to gnaw on come autumn. The taste of hazelnuts in the Christmas ale is not to be sneezed at. One must be mindful of not drinking it too fast, however, so as not to have them catch in the windpipe. I have drunk ale seasoned with nuts as well as cumin. That was at the time we celebrated Christmas with Dacke† at Bergkvara Hall.

---

* May 25, considered the first day of summer.—Tr.

† Nils Dacke, 1500–43, fervent Catholic and leader of the peasant revolt against King Gustav Vasa, who adhered with equal fervor to the reformation and had, by force, collected heavy taxes and stripped the churches of their riches. Dacke's revolt was initially successful, and the province of

When I served as Dacke's piper, I was sometimes given ale from the noblemen's table. And I have sounded my pipe in the great hall of Bergkvara, home of the Trolle clan.‡ I had not been personally invited to play by the lords—we were all self-invited guests at Bergkvara that Christmas. That did not in any way lessen the magnificence of the banquet in the Trolle hall, however. The Dacke feud was lusty sport then—it grew gruesome and cruel with time. The sport has reached its end now, and Dacke's skull is whitening on a pole in Kalmar, it is rumored. God shall revenge his death and plunge the heretic king into the devil's stewpot.

The coolness from the previous night still lingered under the oak trees. I was so thirsty that my exhalation smoked. I lowered my jug into the water, filled it, and drank. The spring quenched my thirst. I drank till I choked. I drank water out of necessity and was aught ashamed of it afterward. Mayhap I drank more than necessity dictated in order to slake my thirst. It lowers and humiliates a man to be reduced to filling his belly with drink destined for dumb beasts.

I sat down at the spring's edge. The young oaks were giving shelter to a poor, hungry wretch who anon had been drinking water. I pulled some chard with my fingers and chewed on it to ease my hunger pangs. I had neither a chunk of bread nor a morsel of meat in my hut. From my belt hung my coin pouch, empty and awakening naught but annoyance. I noticed that the clasp on the pouch was beginning to rust, as well it might. I could not remember when I last unclasped it to slip a paltry piece of copperplate inside it, not

---

Småland was, for a time, independent and prosperous with Dacke as its ruler. He was eventually killed by Vasa's men and his supporters were either executed or banished.—Tr.

‡ Part of Swedish nobility, 1300–1568. A headless troll appeared on their heraldic shield.—Tr.

to speak of a sterling coin. Who can remember? What use to a man is carrying a pouch that stays forever empty of coins? Why must a man needs drink spring water when God created ale for the quenching of his thirst? Many are the things unfathomable—the riddles without number on this earth.

I, Piper Anders, the finest player of my instrument, the nimblest in the ring of dancers, I go with an empty pouch. I blow my pipe as I lead the dancers. I can clasp a woman's waist with my right hand and the pipe with my left. In these parts of the land, who could do likewise? Who can make each of his two hands perform its own useful task as I can? We have not seen like man yet, and we shan't see him within this reign of the heretic king.

I am both one thing and the other, both spelman and dancing master. The new dance, the Leaping Galliard, which I learned from the Polish kettle-drummer under Dacke, I have taught many men and women, but no one can dance it like I do. What is more, when it comes to the one-legged crane dance and its figures, I am the only skilled dancer among hundreds of botchers and bunglers. Artistry like mine ought by rights to be better esteemed by humankind. Yet, what is it we now hear being acclaimed and touted? The wrestler, the marksman, the cattle-driver who can show off a well-trained team, he is more highly regarded than I, Piper Anders.

What I know about playing and dancing cannot be learned in a day, or in ten years. I was only a tiny barefoot shepherd when I carved my first pipe on the pine-clad sandy heath outside our cottage. I carved it out of a little pine shoot. That is how a spelman should begin. He must fashion his plaything with his own hands, then, he will know it fully. There was not a day during my childhood when I failed to practice on my pine pipe. Later, I carved flutes from other kinds of wood. I played on pipe after pipe until it broke. I played assiduously and tried different sorts of wood. I grew up, and as my lungs grew stronger, I required stronger music makers. Such is the law of nature.

These were the many years of apprenticeship. Now, I am a master. I now possess a pipe made of the finest boxwood. One could say that I can now form my lips around an aperture of the noblest wood, and I have six finger holes, three for each hand. I can use my pipe as I please—with my right hand, with my left hand, with both my hands. And it is not to be mistaken for the grasp used by the farmer to hold the handle of his dung-fork.

All who have heard my pipe are amazed over the variety of sounds I can coax from a piece of wood. As soon as I begin to play at a banquet or dance pavilion, I set in motion all things that are not fastened to the walls. The women jump over high tables and benches to reach the dance floor quickly, and the men take to screaming like stallions in heat. Such is the great power exerted by a piece of boxwood over mankind. Yet only in the hands of Anders, the piper, played by his mouth only, can it exert this power.

My years as a journeyman are finished. Now, I am master. Yet, at my belt hangs a sagging pouch, while many men who can do nothing but find fault with the masterful carry bulging pouches. In this world of envy, in this dwelling of injustice, no one is rewarded according to his merit. In God's heaven only shall I gain my rightful place.

The man who strikes up the tunes and leads the dancers may eat and drink his fill at the banquet. But following the banquet, he needs to eat and drink still. He will need to husband his strength and health in order to be ready when next he is sent for:

"Come, Piper Anders, lead us in the dancing!"

The day may come when I answer:

"Piper Anders lies dead in his hut. We have found his wretched bones—he starved to death from the wages he received for his mastery. Should his cadaver rise up to lead you in the dancing, good men and women?"

I have been summoned to play under the oaks for this Midsummer feast. My body wants strengthening for the evening. Should I, then, be required to satisfy myself with cattle drink from the spring? What likeness was it you created your image from here on earth, my lord?

Our almighty father gave me my body and all my senses. He gave me my sound wits. He gave me my nose, with which I can smell the flowers in the meadow. My eyes that gaze into the depths of the spring are his precious gifts. My neck and throat, he gave me. My fingers that play over the pipe holes were his gifts to me. As well as my arms and legs and other members—the member that commits the mortal sin and pleasures a woman and myself at lovemaking, he has granted me—all this is what the Lord gave me. Yet, the one who gave me my throat has also created the thirst that burns within. Why have I not ale at hand for its slaking, then? The plaguing thirst and the frothing ale, both are part of God's wondrous creation. Why was I given one and not the other?

One day, I shall ask the question of Master Lambert, our parson. He is a wise man and stands upright and courageous for the conviction of his faith. He has not as yet knelt before the heretic king in Stockholm; he follows not the decrees issued by the robber from Upland* and his cohorts. Master Lambert still protects us from spiritual delusion. He is not frightened by what happened to his brother in the priesthood, Master Thord of Älghult, who was also among Dacke's followers and, therefore, was forced to endure being put to the wheel† in Kalmar. In good company was Master

---

* The county in which Stockholm is situated; refers to Gustav Vasa.—Tr.
† Breaking on the wheel was a form of torturous public execution used in the Middle Ages and early modern times in France, Germany, Sweden,

Thord. Like rye sheaves on hay-drying fence posts hung human limbs on the wheels in Kalmar the year the feud ended. There was a time when all who lived in these lands flocked to Dacke—now, no one will openly step forth to declare himself his follower. Master Lambert is the only one to utter the truth. As for me, I am a quiet man of few words who will not say what I think. I do not speak of the Dacke feud; neither do I proclaim to have been part of the sport—I am not one to brag and boast.

Three sorrows have I in this world: regret over my fearful sins is the first. The grief of not having ale on hand when I am thirsty, that is the second. The sad knowledge that Jungfru‡ Brita Spåning loves me not well enough to fulfill my wishes, that is the third. My joys, however, are two only: the happy assurance that my sins have been forgiven through Christ's suffering on the cross is my first one. The joy of having ale at hand when the thirst besets me, that is my second one. Yet, what would be my third happiness in this world, I will not ever gain until the day, or night, when Jungfru Brita fulfills

---

and Russia. The wheel itself was similar to a large wooden wagon wheel, with many radial spokes. The victim was placed on a cart-wheel and his limbs stretched out along the spokes, one by one over two sturdy wooden beams. The wheel was made to slowly revolve, and a large hammer or an iron bar was then applied to the limb over the gap between the beams, breaking the bones. The broken man could take hours, even days, before shock and dehydration caused death. In France, a special grace, called the *retentum*, could be granted, by which the condemned was strangled after the second or third blow, or in special cases, even before the breaking began. Afterward, the victim's shattered limbs were woven ('braided') through the spokes of the wheel, which was then hoisted onto a tall pole, so that birds could eat the sometimes still-living victim.—Tr.

‡ Maid, maiden, virgin. Here, used as an honorific, customary address in Sweden until the eighteenth century for young, unmarried women of noble lineage.—Tr.

my wishes. Whether that day will ever dawn, whether that night will ever fall, God alone can say.

All women, from sensible matrons to tender maidens, will feign be led in the dance by me. Many have been my willing bedmates. Among them, I have as yet encountered no maiden. There have been young maids among them, wearing their hair chastely and respectably bare and loose—yet should not rightly have been allowed to wear it so. Sadness and pain would I feel each time when our bed sporting revealed to me that a woman was not what she made herself out to be. I grieve over the sins of others almost as deeply as over my own. I am not a man to worry over himself only.

One thing have I recognized during my lifetime—woman's promiscuity runs rampant in these times. I have played love's games and had my will with twenty of them or more, but not one of them had her chastity unsullied—with none of them did I find a woman's most precious jewel. Anders, the piper, has not yet had the fortune to be the first with a woman. I have traveled afar; in the course of the Dacke feud, I saw many counties. I am no longer young; I am thirty years of age. Had I been fortunate enough to live in a world of chaste women, I should have been the first with many a young maiden. Master Lambert sighs and frets constantly over the depravity of our times, and I agree with him of all my heart.

Why does a maiden no longer guard her maidenhead? Could she fail to know how highly it is regarded by a man? She may observe it everywhere—how courteously a man will treat a woman he believes to be virtuous and pure. She must know how highly he regards her who by rights wears her hair unbound.

My only question is: Until my dying day, shall I meet nothing but proof of wantonness and fornication? Shall never a maiden be mine? Will I never know with unchallengeable certainty that womanly virtue still exists on this earth?

There is one I love and adore the way one loves and adores the bright lights in the sky. Her, I may touch only while dancing. Jungfru Brita will gladly walk in the ring of dancers with me, but not a step outside of it. She is of rank and wishes to be addressed "Jungfru." That is how we began to address her when her father, Axel Spåning, became reeve of Grimsnäs as Gustav Eriksson's man. That was when the red-coats began swarming over us, and all the traitors who served the heretic king were allowed to don suits of costly broadcloth. Grimsnäs was a fine mansion, stolen from its owner by the king, and Axel Spåning lived there in lavish excess. At the very beginning of the feud, he was struck dead by Dacke's peasants. An axe clove his head the way one splits a piece of wood. Axel Spåning was saved from a worse fate by that stroke of the axe—it came to light that he had given false accounts to the king and accrued the gain from the estate for himself. No one will feel greater outrage at finding himself the victim of theft than a thief, and the great robber from Upland was enraged. He held the relatives of his reeve responsible and forced them to pay. He ran the widow and her children from the estate.

Jungfru Brita and her mother now live on a small, neglected, poor farm which does not yield as much as a pound of butter a year. Jungfru Brita is now almost as poor as I. But she has not yet walked one step outside the ring of dancers with me, given her station. Her distinction, she still carries from her days at the estate. The daughter should not be held accountable for her father's thievery, for I like well the action of the father when he stole goods from a master who is a thousand times more of a thief than he was—a lord who would steal God's holy church silver, who steals royal crowns, entire realms and countries.

Thus, Brita Spåning no longer has a dowry. For that reason, the ranks of her suitors have thinned, for which I am glad. She has hardly had a single suitor since the day Dacke's men split her father's head and the king found that he had been robbed—a lesson that taught him that henchmen will readily do as their masters. Among the lords, no one was eager to wed the daughter of a destitute family, and even their riches are less these days. In the early days of the feud, all rich men feared for their property. Many lords buried their treasures in the ground. So did Lord Krabbe of Kråkesjö and Lord Spoke of Gåsamåla. At Räppe, Lord Krabbe was shot to death, and no one knows where his gold and silver lies hidden. So may God keep the money hoarders from pocketing their heart's desire.

Yet, how many women could I name who own handsome dowries and naught but gold and silver to adorn them? Jungfru Brita, on the other hand, shines rare amongst them. Her forehead is radiant with the honor and virtue that make for a woman's most glorious jewel. Brita is for me the ray of purity that brightens this dark world of depravity and fornication—she is pure as the spring that runs here by the hill.

She is my chief sorrow, my deepest pain, my greatest joy in this world.

Thus, I sat in the morn of yesterday at the foot of the hill, pondering over my woes and delights, when I suddenly made a discovery.

I saw something glimmer at the bottom of the spring. Something white lay down there. I bent down over the water and knit my brows together—it was a coin. A silver coin glittered before my eyes from the depths of the spring.

I lay down in my full length, so that the tip of my nose dipped into the water, and let my eyes sweep the entire surface of the bottom. Wherever I gazed, I saw a spot of light—coins! Some I could see in their entirety, some were partly covered, so that only a piece of them would be visible through the mud. Among the white spots, yellow ones appeared, glowing like buttercup crowns.

The bottom of the spring was covered with coins.

I knew well how the coins had reached the depths of the water. They had been dropped in there in order that the spring would help the givers and fulfill their wishes—cure the lame of his limp, the scabies sufferer of his infested skin, the eyes of the blind, the ears of the deaf, and the poor lass who had lost her chastity in the meadow grass—she would become a maiden once more through the spring's good offices. All the things the spring had done for the people through the years had cost much money, if one counted no more than a hundred years back in time. On the bottom down there, I could well see what it had cost.

I had never been one to throw a coin here. I had heeded Master Lambert who had instilled in us that all sacrifice made to a spring or stream were false beliefs and the worst form of idolatry—the most serious offense against the first commandment, "You shall have no other gods before me." No other sacrifices were permissible except those made to the church of our holy Christ. Not that I had presented any gifts to the church, but I was at least innocent of any part of the idolatry that took place here by the meadow spring. I never concealed or sought to excuse my sins when I went to our parish priest to acquire indulgences for them. I could state with assurance that I never sacrificed to this heathen spring.

Here I saw these wondrous coins glitter and glimmer in the water and sorrowed over man's false beliefs and foolishness. Every coin at the bottom of the spring bore witness of an offense against the church's sacred commandment. This silver and gold shone and glowed to me all the tales of unwise and benighted men and women who put their mortal salvation at risk in order to seek cures for their bodily ills, their limps, their scabies, blindness, their deafness.

They traded a passing pain for the eternal torment. Who in his right mind would not rather limp his way through the short human life than burn forever in hell without ever being consumed by the flames?

How I pitied the poor, misguided young women who doomed themselves to eternal hellfire by seeking to redeem their bodily virtue. It was rumored that they could regain it here in the water for the sake of an innocent young maiden who in heathen times was once sacrificed in the spring. I had observed how deeply this and other false beliefs of the faith grieved Master Lambert. I knew he prayed fervently and said many a mass for these women who sought help from a dead heathen deity. The foolish ones believed that the god truly lived there in the spring water, because it ran north.

Moreover, I felt quite dejected at the thought that the coins lay here at the bottom of the spring to no sensible purpose, to no one's benefit or joy. What good and blessed things could they not buy? They could succor the poor and wretched; they could still the cries of children, dry the widow's tears. They could satisfy hunger and quench thirst.

Not only had the idolaters sinned against their God but against their hungering and thirsting neighbor as well.

And as that thought ended its course through my head, it happened—

Just as I grieved most sorely over the foolishness of humankind, the marvelous inspiration seized me. It came with such force that I gave a start. It was a heavenly summons, a command:

"Piper Anders! Seldom has an opportunity presented itself to you for doing good deeds. Nor often has providence chosen you to be the one to gladden your Lord. Yet, here lays a good deed await-ing a strong, courageous believer in the Church of Christ. Hear your calling—these coins shall no longer lie useless and buried under water, mire, and sludge. They must be harvested and used for a holy and Christian purpose. And you, Piper Anders, have been chosen by God to harvest them. You are the one to clear out the water of the dead old heathen god. No one in this neighborhood has the audacity to do it. Every other man and woman is slave to the belief in the power of the sacred spring. Because of their misguided belief and superstitious fears, they dare not touch these coins with their hands. They view them as the property of the idol and are deeply afeard of his vengeance. But the heathen god is dead and can do you neither harm nor good. You need not fear. You shall take from him the gold and silver that the misguided people gave him in their foolishness. You shall take the money from the idol and give it to the only living god. You shall bring them to Master Lambert who will hold them for the Church of Christ."

The summons seemed at once evident and clear to me: It was our church that was calling me. How paltry, desolate, and denuded was *our* house of God now, after the plundering carried out by the great church desecrator in Stockholm! From our temple, he had stolen the golden effigy of Maid Mary, the mother of God. The day I came into the house of God and did not see her standing by the altar rails, I wept bitter tears. Stealing from churches was the greatest pleasure this heretic king ever knew. Could I have been chosen to avenge the theft from our church? Mayhap the gold and silver from the heathen god could buy back the image of Maid Mary?

Our church was in need of Piper Anders' arm.

I set to work at once. I hesitated not for a moment. I knew from the outset how I must proceed.

I went to my hut and fetched the closely meshed bag net I use for baiting. I had tied it during the long winter nights. I used it to retrieve the fish I caught on my hooks. The fine mesh of the bag net would catch the coins in the spring.

Now, in summer time, the spring ran in its thin flow, but it was near three cubits deep. A full-grown man could lower himself into it completely. I thrust the bag net in. If I added the full length of my arm to that of the bag net handle, I could just about reach the bottom. The spring water soaked my shirt sleeve completely.

The very first plunge of the bag net brought up four coins from the depths. I kept on fishing, rushed and eager. I moved my bag net all the way around inside the spring; the water grew murky and unclear, and I could no longer see the bottom. Yet, each time I lifted the bag net, the glimmering shone through the mesh.

I lay on my stomach above the water hole, panting and fishing, until thrice in a row the bag net came up empty. The spring had been cleaned out.

Now, I sat down to examine my haul. In the grass around the spring, the coins glittered and glimmered, from the silver of the thalers and the gold of the ducats. Among them lay the green and verdigrises copperplate pieces. In addition to all the coins, I had fished from the depth of the spring a weighty, handsome necklace of sterling silver.

I counted the coins to two score and four. There were old coins and new ones, known and unknown. There were the heretic king's new copper square klippings,* and king Kristoffer's old silver marks. I valued each coin separately, weighing it in my hand. A copper klipping was of little value. But there were over one score of sterling silver coins. There were four ducats only, but their gold lay heavy in my hand. And the beauteous necklace must be worth at least forty silver ounces Troy.

* "Klipping = square-shaped coin."—Au.

I was not skilled in assessing the values of these coins, but I could well imagine all the fine farms they might procure. With much pain, I might catch a perch or two, a flaccid pike, or a few eels from the lake for my sustenance. Here, in a short while, I had fished a great fortune out of the spring without much toil.

Many would go to great length, toiling and digging with much diligence for treasures hidden in the soil. They would strive years on end without finding as much as one copperplate piece. When the feud ended, how many had not tried to dig up Lord Krabbe's treasure, hidden away at Kråkesjö—whereas I, without seeking, with no digging, had found a treasure! It showed itself before my eyes, and all I needed to do was dig it up—God surely had a meaning with this find.

The spring had been cleaned out—robbed of its bottom gilding of gold and silver. But it ran its course still, shivering softly in its runnel . . . It had been powerless to prevent me from robbing it of its horde. How foolish of man to put his trust in the spring! The old heathen god was dead.

A pure, heartfelt joy coursed through my heart. This mighty treasure had I, Piper Anders, secured for the church of Christ. I knew, then, the truth in the adage that a good deed is its own finest reward.

I placed the money and the chain inside my leather pouch, causing it to fill up and swell like a perch distended with roe at spawning time. Off to Master Lambert, my revered father confessor. Right in front of him, onto his table, I would pour out the contents of my swelling pouch. "Take this money, Father! I have fished it out of heathen waters! To our sacred church will I deliver them!" And I see Master Lambert's face light up like a candle on the altar ring. He will say: "Piper Anders, my son! It has grieved me to watch how you lived your life; you have been a drunkard, led men and women in unchaste dancing, you gambled, you have copulated with whores and other wanton women. You have confessed your sins to me and received letters of pardon. You have returned to confess still more grave sins. Today, you show the purity of your heart's ruing before me, that your heart feels humility and regret, that your yearning for purity and forgiveness for your sins is true. You are a poor man who found a great fortune with which to fill your pouch. Yet, instead of abandoning yourself to the rich man's life of wasteful luxury and gluttony, you bring your riches to the church! You are a true Christian!"

Thereafter, our well-respected parish priest would embrace me warmly and bless me for a long time before I set out on my return home, my pouch dangling from my belt, just as empty as ever before.

So, that morning early, I set out on my way straight to church with my pouch full of the gold and silver taken from the spring. I had a long walk ahead of me. The weather was cool, and I was in the cheeriest of moods, the spring of purpose in my steps. My feet lifted so lightly, as if I were no longer weighed down with the burden of sin. I walked through the forest, jumped over stones and fallen trees; I might have been leaping in one of my galliards. I did not come a-riding like a gentleman, like any of the cursed red-coats. I never owned a horse. Yet, I was well pleased with things as they were, carried along by the horses of Christ's own apostles—my own strong legs.

By my hip, I felt my heavy pouch dangle, keeping time at every step, and I made up a song to sing while I walked:

"A sinner am I, vice's child. God, I think, shall yet prove mild. Here, to him, I bring gold and silver from the spring."

A piper must know how to make up songs when the need arises. I could do it when I was in a cheerful mood. Many songs had I made up about my beloved, Brita Spåning.

If Master Lambert should wish to reward me in any way for my good deed . . . He was a generous man. Perhaps he might say: "My parishioners are superstitious. No one other than you would have been brave enough to clear out the heathen spring. You deserve some recognition for your great courage. See here, I give you this . . ."

What would he offer me? I felt some doubt—could I rightfully accept any gift? I was not sure about that. I feared that a reward would diminish the pure joy I now felt in my heart.

The sun rose higher. The air turned warmer. My forehead began to run with sweat, and the ground felt burning hot through the tattered bark soles of my shoes. My feet felt heavier, and I started to ponder whether it might be right that I should walk all the way to church without any rest. Should I not grant myself some refreshment on a hot morning such as this?

I had reached the Råstock crossroads. I had come one third of the way. Five steps from the road was Goodwife Dandelion's taproom, where food and drink could be purchased. On the door was a carved figure of a woman holding a firkin of frothing beer in her arms. Goodwife herself stood outside by the wall, the sleeves of her shirt rolled up, scouring her copper kettle in preparation for the holiday. People called her Dandelion because her hair shone bright yellow like a dandelion crown around her head. She was a widow and ran the taproom along with her two daughters, known as "the young roses."*

The Råstock crossroads would be the place where I would get off my feet. As I approached it, it was quite clear to me that I would not have the strength to walk all the way without rest and

* There is a play on words here: the Swedish word for *dandelion* is *maskros*, literally "worm rose." *Ungrosorna,* "the young roses," conveys the relationship with the mother plus a somewhat cavalier way of referring to the young blossoms.—Tr.

sustenance. If I did not still my hunger and quench my thirst, my endurance would simply not last; I would not be able to reach our parish priest with my money. Thus, I must needs stop to catch my breath here out of necessity. It was not to be denied.

And in that instant, I knew precisely what Master Lambert would offer me for my reward—it was a sudden revelation:

"Here, take these copperplate pieces back! Keep them for your own use! You have earned them as an encouragement! Scour them clean and use them with God's blessing!"

With that said, our parish priest would gather the copper coins and put them back in my pouch.

I knew it and had always known it—Master Lambert was a generous and open-handed man. I opened my pouch, picked out all the green and verdigrised copperplate pieces and klipping coins, and put them in my coat pocket. These coins were now mine, and I was keeping them separate from the others since I must in no way have my own money mixed in with the property of the church.

And I knew how very fortunate I was, since I could now buy sustenance for myself at the taproom. I clearly saw God's finger in this—that right at this very moment, I was to have coins of my own in my coat pocket. It could not have been more auspicious.

I entered the taproom, which Goodwife Dandelion's two daughters, Märta and Ingeborg, were busy festooning for the holiday. They put birch branches on the walls and hung flower wreaths on the ceiling beams. The floor had been recently scoured with fine, flour-white sand. The young roses looked askance at my wretched, dusty shoes. They were white-complexioned taproom girls, firm and plump of limbs. That neither of Mistress Dandelion's daughters was a maid, I had had occasions a-plenty to learn.

At this early morning hour, Jakob, the blacksmith, was the only other guest in the taproom. He glared at me with eyes quite still, like those of a dead fish. He seemed more than half drunk; maybe he had been sitting here since yesterday eve.

The dandelion herself came in. Her bloom had passed as far as love's sport, but in her youth, she had not been one to spare herself.

She greeted me, the corners of her mouth lowered.

"Are you offering to play for a jug of ale, Piper Anders?"

"I am to play this night at the festival tree. Now, I mean to pay, both for one and two jugs."

"Ah, do we sound grand," said the dandelion.

"No grander than I am good for," said I and sat down on the bench, my legs spread wide apart.

On the other side of the room sat Jakob the blacksmith, spreading his legs so wide that the taproom girls tripped over them. Was I less entitled than he?

Mistress Dandelion noticed the swelling pouch on my belt.

"What frippery do you carry in your pouch?"

"That is none of your concerns, dandelion!"

It vexed me that she believed me not in a position to carry good money in my pouch.

Goodwife Dandelion pointed to the middle beam in the ceiling where my old beer debits were chalked up in red—two long chalk lines and four short ones, two firkins and four jugs.

She said scornfully:

"Methinks your debt weighs heavy on you?"

Now, it was my turn. Without saying a word, I took all the copper coins out of my coat pocket and laid them on the table. I handled them disdainfully, as if they were nothing but horse dung I'd found on the road. I then contrived it so the clasp of my pouch happened to spring open, so that silver and gold could be glimpsed.

"Strike off my debt! Hand me some ale!"

Mistress Dandelion's nose grew in her face one inch, a long inch. Her eyes flew open and shone tallow yellow. She beckoned to her daughter, Märta, who came forth and brought me ale. I stretched a handful of coins toward Mistress Dandelion, but she refused to accept them. Her sour smile had turned sweet as honey, the smile of obsequious scraping and bowing.

"Drink ere you pay, Piper Anders! You shall have as much credit as you please here, just tell that lass of mine!"

Then, she grasped a hare's foot and rubbed out my six red lines from the ceiling beam. With that, all my indebtedness in all this wide world was obliterated. For on this day, my debt to our father in heaven was to be paid also.

I blew away the foam that frothed over the rim of the tankard. I drank. I felt like a free man.

Mistress Dandelion remained standing by me. She had not been able to take her eyes off my pouch.

"How have you come by all your money, Anders?"

"Are you in the habit of asking such a question to all who enter here, or to me alone? Is it so far from your mind to think that Piper Anders' money was come by honestly?"

I was deeply insulted and let Mistress Dandelion gaze on my back. I did not want to reveal to her that I carried the property of Christ's church in my pouch. I had made a vow not to reveal my feat of this morning to anyone, with the exception of our parish priest. How I despised those who strutted around bragging and boasting of their noble, Christian deeds! Should anyone give a lice-ridden sheepskin to our church, he would be powerless to conceal it. But I would give several farms' worth—I would show them that good deeds could be done and remain hidden.

Mistress Dandelion mumbled conciliatory words—she had merely meant to suggest that I had stumbled upon a treasure. With that, she left the room.

The young rose, Märta, poured more ale into my tankard without my asking, and she also brought me a bowlful of cabbage gruel with boiled pork. My stomach was screaming with hunger. I ate, and I drank. Through my head rang the soothing, comforting fizz of the ale. Through the opening in the wall, I could see the June blossoms carpeting the ground behind the cottage.

I pulled the thickest ducat out of my pouch, rolled it across the table, and listened to the high-pitched clang of the gold. And I said to myself:

"Is that you, Piper Anders, sitting here playing with a farm, with two perhaps?"

I felt like a lord.

The taproom girl, Märta, watched my play with the ducat. She kept glancing at the heavy silver chain in my pouch, cringing and fussing over me. I had had my will with her a few times, and I knew that other men had enjoyed her favors after me. Yet, she wore her hair loose and uncovered like the chastest of maidens.

My eyes saw the taproom girl, Märta, but my thoughts were with Jungfru Brita. With Brita, no man had as yet had his wish fulfilled, with her, no one had had his will. Should a man's eyes as much as gaze at that maiden, her cheeks would color blood red. So behaved a chaste woman if a man were to gaze at her and think that her apple-round breasts would be his sweetest delights in lovemaking.

But this sore trial on this earth had God given Piper Anders— no maidenhead would ever be granted me. My third joy would never be mine; Jungfru Brita would never be mine; never would my dearest one ease my heart.

Yet, the thought that woman's virtue still could be found in this world warmed me. The knowledge that one maiden still existed who bided her man gave me strength. And I thanked God that Jungfru Brita Spåning walked the wondrous earth of his creation.

I drank my ale, blowing the foam away, so sweet and enticing against my lips—to break at the merest touch. It promised to love my mouth, but was nothing but the bubbles of deception, fleeting and vanishing. Like the foam head on the ale, such was your wretched, transient life. The moment you brought it to your mouth to taste it, it ran away between your lips.

Jakob the blacksmith walked up to me and asked if I wanted to throw the dice with him. He had noticed that I sat there with coins in my hands.

Willingly would I play a game of dice for the sake of amusement and to pass the time. However, Jakob the blacksmith was a man deeply in debt and with a wife and ten children to feed. I thought it unwise of him to stake his money on the dice. It was the rightful property of his creditors that he was risking. But Jakob was stubborn, and since one should never unnecessarily provoke another human being, I acquiesced. I still retained all my copper coins, which Mistress Dandelion ought to have taken as payment for my debt. These coins I could well afford to stake!

In the corner stood an old drum which we moved to stand in front of the bench, whereupon we made ourselves comfortable, each with one of the dice. We agreed to stake one klipping each on three throws.

At the first throw on the drum, I showed five holes, Jakob three.

"First game, highest to blame," said we in unison.

Yet, the prophecy did not bear out today. The second throw showed six holes for me, two for Jakob the blacksmith. Of the first nine times I threw, I won seven. Jakob must lay three copper klippings in my pile of money.

My wondrous luck persisted. Three times out of four, I had the highest throw on the drum. Jakob's money pile kept shrinking while mine grew larger. Before today, I would play at the dice for days and night, always losing. But, no matter how I threw the dice on this day, I would invariably show at least one more hole than Jakob. I began to throw quite carelessly, barely lifting my hand, letting the die fall willy-nilly on the drum—I won.

Everything I did was lucky today. I felt like a king.

Jakob the blacksmith was at first annoyed, then suspicious, and, finally, enraged. He wondered if the devil had sold me my gambler's luck in exchange for my soul. He smelled treason and wanted to change dice.

He took my die, I took his. I won as before.

Thus, I played Jakob the blacksmith destitute of all his money, and he began screaming and cursing—he cursed me as well as Mistress Dandelion, her daughters, and her taproom:

"Nest of lice! Den of thievery! Whorehouse!"

All his klippings and copperplate pieces now lay in my pile of winnings. I spoke my honest mind to Jakob, telling him he had done wrong to engage in the game of dice when he was so deeply in debt and had a wife and children to feed. He ought to have remembered that he was the father of a family ere he allowed himself to be made destitute and shamed himself with his gambling and frivolity.

At my gentle remonstrance, Jakob retaliated with still more gross insults, swore by the Lord and his mother, and challenged me to wrestle with him. But I would wrestle with no one who spoke the Lord's name in blasphemy. Jakob then aimed his foot as though to kick me—it struck the drum which crashed noisily across the cottage floor.

Mistress Dandelion came in and threw Jakob the blacksmith out of the taproom, grasping him by the scruff of his neck and picking him up as though he had been no heavier than a young rabbit.

I counted my winnings from the game—six copper klippings, four copperplate pieces, and two sterling silver thalers. All the coins from the meadow spring were blessed—I had but to touch them for them to breed and propagate. I did not wish to keep all the winnings, so I divided them into two equal parts, one to keep for my own use, the other I placed in my pouch along with the money I was to deliver to the church. It was late in the day by now; I ought to be on my way and complete my errand with our parish priest. But it was an oppressively hot day, and I felt tired and weak; I realized that I must rest some before continuing my walk.

I went out behind the taproom, and there, within the leafy shrubbery, I found a luxuriant bush that promised some shade, and here, I lay down to sleep. With no worry to my conscience, I would now be able to gain a few moments of rest. Had I not served God's church even while taking my refreshment in the taproom?

I had added six klippings, two pieces of copperplate, and one sterling silver thaler to the property of the church.

As I awoke, dusk had already fallen. The sun was hidden behind the treetops. I had slept too long to be able to complete my errand to our priest on this day. Ere I could reach my destination, Master Lambert would already have sought his bed, and I was loath to disturb the pious man at his rest. I saw God's design clearly— had it been his intention that I should reach the church with the coins today, he would have awoken me sooner. He would have let a branch or pinecone drop on my head.

Now, I must head elsewhere—the time had come for Piper Anders to play at the Midsummer feast at the dancing meadow.

Thus, I headed back the same way I had come. As I reached the hill, a great number of people were already gathered under the oaks.

The fir tree had been trimmed and was ready to be hoisted. They had been eagerly awaiting my arrival and greeted me with cheerful cries—now, the playing and dancing could soon begin.

My eyes at once sought the one person, and I greeted Brita Spåning with great courtesy. She said she had been waiting for me. Yet, I knew that her words referred only to this night and held true only within the ring of dancers. Silently, I bowed to her.

The largest number of young lads and maidens had assembled at the gathering place in the meadow. The shepherd of our church had in vain admonished the young not to stay outdoors in the open on Midsummer's Night, knowing so well its dangerous power and hold. Fervently, he would preach against the wantonness that reigned outside in God's nature during the shortest night of the year. They desecrated God's image, all those who came together in their heat and whoredom like mindless beasts in the meadows, fields, and ditches. His sermons would not keep the young away from the dancing field—for one night each year, they would stay outdoors, keep their vigil, and do all that was at other times forbidden.

Here were the victuals for the feasting already set out under the oaks. The procurers had walked from farm to farm for days, collecting food and drink, which now was freely offered to one and all. Before the feud, we'd cook a two-year-old bullock and consume the entire carcass at the Midsummer feast. Now, most of our working oxen went to the robber in Stockholm, who had also taken from us the fattest pork from our acorn-fed swine. The heretic king would not be sated unless God filled his mouth with a shovelful of earth—thus we were to reward him with our oxen and swine for his theft of our church silver. Yet, there was no shortage of food to fill our bowels at this feast—boiled long sausages, smoked eels, round, glistening cheeses. There were rows of crocks filled with sweet porridge and honey griddle cakes, brought to the feast by the women. The eggs had been gathered by the procurers, collecting a half-score at each farm. We men pricked holes in the raw eggs and sucked and drank as we had always done this night, for it gave man strength to drink them as they were laid right out of the hen's ass. We then gathered the empty eggshells and strung them up onto the Midsummer tree, which was about to be hoisted.

And the beer was drawn off and flowed from kegs and firkins.

I satisfied my hunger thoroughly and emptied a good half-score of eggs. Following that, I set about trying my pipe. I discovered that some dirt had settled in the mouthpiece as I lay sleeping in that bush. I needed to spend some time cleaning it out; I must blow my pipe pure and sweet for the dancing.

The time came for us men to raise the fir tree up. At its top, we fastened a ram's head with large, glossy eyes. As the Midsummer tree was hoisted, men and women sang as one:

"A tree we raise to the summer sky,
O'er hamlet, roof, and ridge, up high;
A tree we set into the earth,
To fruit and corn in ear, give birth.
Come, young and old! Each one is first
To still his hunger, slake his thirst.
Guests one and all, come and partake!
Midsummer merry we shall make."

The fir tree with its white ram's skull atop it stood high against the sky. We clasped hands and formed a ring and trod the dance around the Midsummer tree and altar. I was the one to lead them, sounding my pipe.

To begin with, my playing sounded somewhat strained. The food I had just taken lay heavy in my bowels, and, time and again,

I found myself needing to burp. There was an occasion or two when the burping occurred so importunately as to interfere with a note, necessitating my removal of my mouth from the mouth hole for a second or two. But by the time that the leaping galliard came around, the food had sunk down sufficiently so that one might, from the sound of the music, recognize the skills of Piper Anders.

While I led the dancers, I was the foremost around the Midsummer tree. This night, I was valued and well regarded—I was indispensable.

"Play, Piper Anders! Play and blow your pipe! No one is your equal tonight. The dancing around the Midsummer altar cannot take place without you. Tonight, you are the master of the playing and dancing! Your pipe moves the ring of dancers across the meadow grass, easy as a rolling wheel! Man and woman, goodwife and maiden, will hop to obey the command of your pipe! At the sounding of your pipe, you will lead the ring games, dance circles, the leaping galliards. Your pipe holds the power that, this night, holds the world.

"So, take your pleasure! Enjoy the happiness of being indispensable! Play! Dance! Strike up your tunes, Piper Anders!"

Oh, I played, I danced, and I blew my pipe with every ounce of breath in me as the night drew near over the young oaks on the hill. On our fir tree, the emptied eggshells hung and dangled like apples on the apple tree branches. At my hip hung my skin pouch, incessantly beating the time as I danced, and it was not empty.

As I began playing the one-legged crane dance, every woman wanted to be partnered by me. I went with Jungfru Brita, and she seemed as eager to dance with me as I with her.

Facing one another, we hopped, each on one leg. We changed legs and hopped again, and Brita said it gave her great pleasure to dance with me. I wondered if the day would ever come when she would address me so sweetly outside the ring of dancers. But her station would in all likelihood forbid her ever to do so.

We danced the one-legged crane dance for as long as our endurance allowed. Brita's eyes were tender as she looked at me. As my gaze touched hers, her cheeks changed their hue. This much I dared surmise—she was not indifferent to me.

I shifted my purse so it rested behind my back. With its girth, it proved uncomfortable in the one-legged crane dance. It leaped up toward Jungfru Brita's bodice and hit her in the stomach a few times, which caused me much embarrassment. I entreated the maid to forgive the uncouth comportment of my purse. As fortune would have it, she did not prove outraged by it.

"Is it gold and silver you carry in your pouch," asked Brita.

"Some gold, I might have," I answered.

"Then, you are a happy and well-off man, Piper Anders," she asked.

"Today, since this morning, I have felt happy," I said.

Jungfru Brita became curious and asked me many a question as regarding the gold in my pouch, but I still kept my silence concerning my exploit of this morning at the spring—I held true to my decision not to boast. But once the one-legged crane dance was at an end, I opened my pouch and showed her my ducats.

She was deeply amazed at the handsome coins she saw in there.

"Are these the coins of the sun? Are these golden wheels?" Jungfru Brita asked.

"They glitter like Fairwheel, our sun," I retorted.

"Are these coins part of a treasure?"

"You could be guessing right!"

She grew keener:

"You must tell me . . . Have you dug up Lord Krabbe's treasure or Lord Spole's?"

"Neither. More, I cannot tell you."

But no matter what I said, Jungfru Brita remained convinced that I had found noblemen's gold, buried in the earth at the time of the feud. And, since I wished not to engage in self-boasting, I could not reveal the truth—that the treasure was the property of the church. She now surmised that the money belonged to me, and naught could I do to prove otherwise.

"You need tell me nothing," she whispered and leaned close to my ear. "My eyes can see."

Once more, we danced. Egad, she was not high-minded toward me this night; she showed me more favor than she ever had in the ring of dancers. I became giddy with wonderment. Within me, the question swelled—the most audacious, the foolhardiest, the one never even hinted at—was I dear to her?

She had seemed to wish to share my secrets. And whom should I take into my confidence if not her? It plagued me to keep anything hidden from Brita.

As soon as seemed opportune, I took the beautiful silver chain out of my pouch and held it up to her eyes.

"A necklace," she cried, "silver chain."

"Pledge silver," I answered.

"Is it yours?" she asked.

"It is in my keeping," I said.

Jungfru Brita's eyes remained fixed on the necklace for a long time. Quietly, she stammered:

"Silvern chain! Silvern chain! . . ."

The necklace would likely be worth at least one hundred lod, but I said nothing of it—and no interest had Jungfru Brita in what money the silver might fetch. She rejoiced in its beauteous glow. Yet, why should her eyes alone delight in the pleasure of the necklace? Why should they not let her hands share in the delight?

I could let her hold it—who should be entitled to do so if not her, my confidante, my beloved?

And I lay the silver necklace in Jungfru Brita's hand. Her hands caressed the silver.

The night began to turn light.

The crowd was dispersing. The young people were scattered everywhere throughout the meadow. The feasting at the Midsummer tree was over. The sun would soon be rising.

Jungfru Brita and I were standing neath one of the oaks on the hill. It had happened! It had happened—she had taken her first step outside of the dancers' ring with me.

And her eye sought mine, and her countenance was a rosy, warm cloud. Why would all this be happening if I were not dear to her?

I had put away my pipe of boxwood and ceased playing. I reflected on all these years and days I had been carrying my deepest wish. I had asked Jungfru Brita if she, too, had a deepest wish, and she had given me no answer. Yet, she had lowered her gaze at the question.

In my hand lay the heavy chain of silver which she had gazed upon and returned to me. My eyes rested on her neck, which shone white and lovely in the darkness. There was the right, soft bed for the silver chain. Why should she not wear the silver necklace on this night? What difference did it make if the church's silver lay in my pouch or around her neck? No difference whatsoever did it make. It would be as securely kept at either place.

Quietly and without a word, I raised my hands over her head. Carefully, with trembling hands, I lay the silver chain around Jungfru Brita's neck.

I felt her bosom heave.

"Is it pledge silver?" she said.

"I said it anon," I said. "It is pledge silver."

Thereupon, we walked slowly across the meadow. I did not ask her to come with me. She did so without my urging. I had but to walk across the field, and she followed.

How far would Jungfru Brita go with Piper Anders outside of the dancers' ring?

She kept fingering the chain around her neck. The silver moved and lived its life in the glow. And she followed me, walked by my side.

We walked past the spring, purling in its runnel. Something about the sound of the running spring bade me to pause and listen. Yet, I had completed my task; I had no further errand here. I wanted nothing from the spring this night. I walked on; I did not pause.

How far would Jungfru Brita follow me outside of the dancers' ring? I already knew: she would follow me as far as it pleased me, as far as I would go, for I was dear to her.

We reached a flat space in the shelter of a large oak tree. The grass was silky and soft there, very little dew had fallen on it, and that is where we stopped.

So, at last, came the third joy to Piper Anders, shortly before sunrise.

You did not halt by the spring, Piper Anders! Had you paused to listen, you would have been told, you would have been warned. You ought to have listened.

The spring purls:

"Piper Anders, who is it that gave you the maiden in your arms? Wherefrom did you gain the power over Jungfru Brita?

"The sun lord, my god, still sleeps in his chamber on this, the shortest night of the year. It is his awesome night, the sacrificial night of the virgin brides. Then, my deity's power rises from my depths. Then, he is master; then, he will breach the maiden's shield, the most precious tissue ever spun around the earth. Then, the blood will be sacrificed to the soil. Life sacrifices to itself in order to remain. It shall remain for as long as it keeps sacrificing to itself.

"My deity has bestowed its power on me tonight. I cure the blind man's eye, the deaf man's ear, the lame man's leg, the scabby skin of the scabies sufferer. And I will heal once more the maiden who sacrifices her blood at the feast of the virgin brides—cleansed in my water, she will walk from hither in the morning sun with her hair loose, the sign of the untouched.

"When the sun last rose, the bright lights of gold and silver still shone in my depth. That was the sacred treasure, my lord's property. It was the treasure amassed out of faith, devotion, prayers, wishes that human beings had proffered. These were the tributes of the faithful, and they hold power.

"Yet, shortly after sunrise, while the oak trees shaded my water, cool and fresh in the morning, a robber happened by. He used force, he plundered my womb, he extinguished my lights, and he desecrated my shrine. Now, no lights of gold and silver glimmer within my depth. Now, there is nothing but mud, moraine, gravel, and stone. My depth is dark as the night.

"For as long as my deity remains concealed in his sleeping chamber, the robber's luck will hold. For now, may he use my silver and have his will with the maiden. Have your happiness while you may, Piper Anders! Here, right near your bed of lovemaking, sings I, the plundered spring, and I ask: 'Wherefrom hast thou gained power over Jungfru Brita?' From me have you stolen it. Return it you shall. I run north, to where my god is. Soon, the sun will rise once more, and you will lose your spoil. You shall see. The sun god will then reclaim his sacred treasure.

"You ought to have stopped and listened to me, Piper Anders!"

I had my pleasure with Brita, my sweeting, under the large oak where the grass was not harsh and rough. Our pleasure did not hurry its departure. For the first time ever, I could delight in a maiden and enjoy her pure innocence. Long was I with her, and I was happy to teach Brita that her breasts also were part of the games that man and woman play with each other; and the bliss of our embraces remains with me in the knowledge that she would henceforth belong to me.

Long afterward, I kept caressing her. I said:

"Three things are round, Brita—the sun, the coins of gold, and your breasts."

She gave no answer to that. I know not whether she found the words discourteous, but she began fastening her bodice. Inside the bodice, she enclosed her breasts, red and swollen like ripening rosehips after our lovemaking.

The silver chain fell like sun glints over water from her neck down over her breasts. Seldom did her hands leave it—constantly, she stroked the heavy links of the chain.

Then, she said:

"Anders, tell me—now, you need no longer keep it a secret from me—whose treasure did you unearth? Where did you find it? Please tell!"

Should I persist in keeping my secret even from her, who had now become my true love? With what creature upon this earth was I to share it, if not with her? Could I not tell her the truth without resorting to bragging and self-boasting?

"I have cleaned out the spring," I said, holding back out of my voice all pride and delight over my exploit.

"Of what spring do you speak?"

"The one right here by the hill."

"The sacred spring . . . ?"

"She has been thus called."

Brita had lingered over her last words, and, wondering, I looked up at her face.

"Does your gold and silver come from the sacred spring?"

I nodded.

"And the necklace . . . ?"

"All has been taken from the spring."

The pallor of her cheeks terrified me. Before I could cry out, she herself uttered a scream:

"God help me!"

She stood up vehemently and cried as though suffering the agony of death:

"God, help me! God, help me!"

With both hands, she grasped the silver chain and drew it over her head, trembling as if the cold scales of a snake were touching her neck. She threw the necklace far from her—I saw it fall into the grass.

"Brita, what has come over you?"

"May our almighty god help me! I wore that chain!"

"What harm have you wrought in doing so?"

"You stole it from the sacred spring! I have worn the pledged silver chain. God help us both!"

Jungfru Brita fell into heart-rending sobs. While she sobbed, she accused me—how could I not have known what I was doing? Who was I not to have known this:

Whosoever removes or touches the gifts sacrificed to the spring also takes upon himself all the torments that the givers were spared.

Here I stood, my coin pouch swollen with the gifts from the spring of the heathen god. Beside me in this meadow stood a betrayed and sobbing maiden.

The sun had risen.

Jungfru Brita wept her tears and kept accusing me.

I had cheated and betrayed her. I had allowed her to believe that I had found and dug up a lord's treasure. I had pretended to be another than what I was—a rich man—and I had betrothed her to me and given her pledge silver that belonged to the spring. Believing herself honorably betrothed to an honest man, she had abandoned her virtue and let me near her. In good faith had she worn the pledged silver from the sacred spring around her neck. What would now befall her? Would she now have to await blindness, deafness, scabies, and lameness? Would she now have to endure all the plagues that the sacrificers had escaped and left in the water of the spring?

Jungfru Brita named me traitor, deceiver, maidenhead thief, and robber of maidens.

Where I stood, sorrow bowed my head. What had I done to Brita? What had she done to me? Indeed, may God have pity on Brita Spåning! May our God help Piper Anders! Wretched man! How soon did not the third joy flee from you!

There, right before my eyes, stood truth and told me: You were never dear to her.

And yonder, in the grass, a necklace lay gleaming like a silver snake.

Jungfru Brita never was mine. It was the treasure that had power over her, not I. It was to the spring's gold and silver that she gave herself, not to me. The silver and gold were not mine—that is why Jungfru Brita cries.

Who did I think I was just then, when the treasure was supposed to have been mine? The heir to Lord Krabbe—to Lord Spole? Now do you see who you are, when nothing but the truth counts? You are an able player and dancer, Piper Anders, but naught else. Therefore, no woman wants you for a husband.

I took what she gave me for love. It seemed to me as though her heart opened and came near to mine. I thought she wished to come into the arms of the one she loved. Now, it was clear to me that love had never been part of our embraces. I embraced my sweeting, and she embraced my coin pouch.

Thus, our intercourse turned into a bad bargain between us— the worst bargain I ever entered into on this earth. Nothing but intercourse between an unmarried woman and an unmarried man had occurred—simple whoring, that was all.

Who would now comfort the maiden who cries her tears into the meadow? Who would now comfort my desolate heart?

The third joy had passed, and in its stead, my fourth sorrow appeared.

In the grass, the circle of the snake lay glittering under the rays of the sun. It was the silver snake that had lain around her neck. It was that snake that had lured Jungfru Brita and desecrated her.

Then, the Lord spake to the woman:

"Why hast thou done it?"

The woman answered:

"The snake deceived me, so that I ate."

Yet, Jungfru Brita blames me. She claims I am the one who treated her so cruelly, that I have dishonored her, my dearest one. I desired my sweeting—was that wrong of me?

The silver snake lay in its circle in the grass, glistening. Brita had shrieked and shrunk back as she saw it entwined around her throat—and I was the one who had hung it around her neck.

Brita was a maid without means, the daughter of one of the king's thieving overseers. When man adorned her with pledge silver, she accepted it. Was she wrong to do so?

She cried:

"All imaginable torments are attached to your gold and silver! Rid yourself of it all! Put it back in the spring!"

"Put it back! No, that I will not do."

I glanced over at the shining, white-scaled snake there on the ground, who had betrayed Jungfru Brita. Was it raising its head and showing its fang? A very short while ago, it had been a silver necklace, which I had lent my sweeting. Why did I not go and retrieve the necklace? Could it be that I feared the god that lived in the north, in the direction of which the spring runs?

Jungfru Brita was frightened of the heathen god, and she was trying to frighten me. But I would show her that he was no longer powerful.

I stood up and went over to where the silver snake lay in the grass and picked it up. It lay limp and still in my hands, it did not wriggle around my fingers, no adder pierced my flesh. It was no snake, but a silver necklace, worth well over forty silver ounces Troy.

For the second time this night, I held the necklace up to Jungfru Brita's eyes:

"Still your tears! See here, there is no evil in this silver."

But at that, she let out a scream of horror and ran away.

She fled . . . She was gone. In my hand, she had seen nothing but the golden snake that had deceived her. I put the heavy silver chain back into my pouch.

Thus ended the evil maidenhead bargain between my sweeting and me in the night of the Midsummer feasting—we were both fooled.

The crowd had dispersed and had left the Midsummer feast in the meadow. My sweeting was gone, and I alone was left. The sun had risen, and I reflected on the deeds I had done while the last day and night sped through its circle. I had been drinking and gambling, I had been playing and dancing, I had committed adultery and dishonored a maiden, my dearest one. I began to grieve and mourn—the new day was shedding its light on a great sinner.

Now, what would befall Jungfru Brita? She was dishonored. No help could she seek in the old spring, which had lost its power, though the simple fools who put their faith in her still were numerous. She would have to wear her unbound hair like a false maiden. The king had made her family destitute, yet mayhap a suitor would come to her, a man with a homestead. He might say:

"I will have you without dowry. Would you be my bride come autumn?"

Her mother would be happy, and Brita would gratefully accept his offer. By the time of the autumnal equinox, her bridal sheets would be spread in the bed. But it was a false virgin bride who rode with her groom to church and priest to the accompaniment of music and drums. On the morning after, the groom's mother would inspect, as any groom's mother, suspicious of her son's wife, has been wont to do through all times—she would inspect the sheets used during the night.

"Not a drop. No, not one red drop on the sheets! By the sun and the moon and all God's holy angels, not one single drop! My son has been made a fool of. My family has been shamelessly deceived. This Jungfru Brita comes into our home without as much as a spoon for a dowry, and she has the gall to deceive us to boot! Perhaps the whore is set on implanting bad blood into our family. My son, what will you do?"

How harsh, of a sudden, will be the voice of the groom—the tender husband of the past night. See, now, he is a man deeply wronged. What does he know? Perhaps his bride is already a faded bride who will bear a child before her time—an autumn bride who gives birth in the spring? What does he know? And no honorable and family-proud man will suffer foreign blood to inherit his house and land.

So she will be driven out of the house, she, who was yesterday's false bride. She will be driven out to wander the roads among disreputable women. Among the poor drifters and vagabonds, she will now find her rightful place. She is perhaps carrying a child that sucks at her nipples as she begs for food and water. This is the offspring of Piper Anders suckling a beggar woman. It is Piper Anders' child being raised among drifters and loose rabble.

The cause of all this evil is none other than I. I had desired Jungfru Brita, but the desire was rooted in pride and lust—a lecher's desire. What happened between us was nothing better than an act of sin; and I had been the tempter, the seducer. Thus, the truth stared me in the face, spoken with our parish priest's mouth:

"You have run about in the night of mortal sin and been governed by your whorish heat in the meadows and fields!"

I regretted my misdeeds, I grieved over all the wrong I had done. I sat down at the root of the oak tree and felt my regret weigh down on me like lead and stone. I had wished no evil, had never wanted to cause any harm to my neighbor, and for my sweeting, I had wanted the best only. Yet, I had wrought evil.

Our morning sun lit its fire in the tops of the oak trees over my head. The dew of health covered the ground all around. The birds had begun singing in the bushes from all directions. Here I sat in the midst of the meadow on the morning bursting with life at its fullest, knowing that I was bound for hell.

The grass smelled sweet like cumin loaf in my nostrils. I was right within a vibrant green herb garden, and in all branches and treetops, the birds gave forth their own music, God's own pipes. And I, God's image, was the most wretched man that a green tree ever sheltered on this earth—the lowest of creatures, a befouled image of God—a pathetic excuse of a man on his way to hell and who had managed to cover a good portion of his journey thither on this night.

I knelt against the oak, I folded my hands in prayer, and I cursed myself and my desires. Tears sprang out of my eyes, stinging like the bitterest salt. They were the burning tears of my remorse. Such tears had I wept on many occasions, usually at morning-time.

I prayed to our God. From this lovely morning on, I would change my way of life. Beginning with the very sunrise that now shed its light upon this meadow, I would destroy the lustful being inside my body and soul. After this night of mortal sin, I would never again perform my tunes for playing and dancing. Never again would I lead the ring of dancers. After this night, no one would ever more hear me play my pipe, leading the young in wanton dances. Piper Anders would be Piper Anders no more.

I was headed for hell. At this moment, I would turn about. I would take the quickest road to God's house, to our parish priest, Master Lambert, and confess to him my grave transgressions. If I went there right away, I should reach him at the hour when he rose from his bed. I would at once tell him all I had done during the night of mortal sin, and he would issue me a letter of pardon and forgiveness. Once the blood of Christ had washed away my sins, I would tell to him my second errand. I would hand over my money pouch to Master Lambert, into which I would lay every coin, sterling, as well as copperplate, not one copper klipping would I keep for myself. And I would say:

"This is my gift to the church of Christ, rescued from the spring hole of the heathen god. I have been carrying this pouch all day round and all night, but I have wasted or misappropriated nothing. Instead, I have added six klippings, two copperplates, and one thaler sterling silver."

Naught would I keep for myself. All would be used for the benefit of Christ's church. This gift would help bring back the picture of God's gentle mother, Maid Mary, inside the altar ring of our Lord's temple. And I, having destroyed my former being, would see all my sins eradicated; I would no longer be Piper Anders, spelman and dancing master.

I reached for my pipe to break and destroy it. My pipe of precious boxwood was a tool tarnished with sin and must be broken. I levered it against my knee.

Of a sudden, my hands grew still. My dear old instrument, my pipe—was this necessary? Could I not transform this instrument of sin into an instrument of God? Could I not blow my pipe in the service of God and use my skill for the praising of the Lord?

This was an inspiration that I felt I could trust—if, from now on, I used my pipe to produce sounds for the sole purpose of honoring and praising God, I would still be granted permission to use it. King David was allowed to play his harp as much as he wanted to. Lowly and wretched man that I was, God would surely allow me to play my pipe

The decisions I had just made eased my mind. I would have felt quite fine had a severe thirst not come over me. I would eventually grow thirsty from ale already drunk, from the ale I had drunk this night and yesterday. So, I began to wander around and look within the bushes on the hill, where the feasting crowd had been eating and drinking. I reckoned that a jugful of ale might have been left at the bottom of some vessel left behind.

I searched diligently and found a firkin, hidden and forgotten inside a hazel thicket. Liquid still gurgled inside the vessel. I put my mouth to the tap hole and drank. What bliss to slake my burning thirst with the cool ale, though it tasted somewhat flat from having stood overnight. I lay down on my stomach in the hazel thicket and rested. Now and then, I put my lips to the firkin and drank.

Soon, complete calm had settled within my mind, and I felt great well-being. Mayhap I had felt some awe before the heathen god when Jungfru Brita claimed that I had gathered all the world's torments in my pouch. Now, however, I knew myself to be secure under the protection of the only true god. I had shed my morning tears; I felt reassured and calm.

And I listened to the music from branch and treetop, which had been heard from the firmament ever since the fifth day when the waters issued forth all their flying and crawling animals, and God created his feathered pipes, the throats of the birds. The longing to join in and play now seized me, and I was relieved not to have broken my pipe in my fervor of a few moments ago. A soiled image of our Lord I might be, a wretched ne'er-do-well I might well be, yet, amongst all these winged creatures, I wanted to give voice to God's heavenly creation this Midsummer morning.

So, my lips blew once more, my hands played over the finger holes. From within the hazel bush, I joined my voice to that of thrush and passerine, finch and cuckoo, wren and pied flycatcher, and all the other winged creatures.

"I play my morning song on my pipe
While flies, bees, and bumblebees buzz and drone
And the ant scurries forth with pine-needle and straw, each one
'Round the tree stump grey, the anthill to raise
Southward they hasten in the sunshine.

And the thyme glows red at the edge of the field,
Red as the blood-stained sin of mine.
And from inside her sleep-chamber shield
The sun has awakened to shine.
For the shortest night on this earth did she rest
In the north, where she has her shrine.
She shines on the sinner once more.
The bird sings out from a jubilant breast
All creatures join in the song
All will be silent, come night, hence they draw
Tomorrow anew, their sound in praise
Will flow again, all day long
While flies, bees, and bumblebees buzz and drone
And I play my morning song on my pipe."

I must not linger overlong at my playing, however. I must quickly be on my way to our parish priest in order to reach him before mass.

I drank the last swigs out of the firkin. The comforting buzz of the ale rose up into my head. Standing up, I found myself not quite steady on my legs. I was, perhaps, somewhat intoxicated from the ale gone flat overnight. I would be able to walk off the intoxication on my way to church. Today, my thirst had been slaked early in the morning—no need to stop at Goodwife Dandelion's taproom. From my belt hung my coin pouch, just as heavy and swollen as before, striking my thigh as I began to walk.

I put the pipe to my lips and blew. Thus, I quickened my body and lightened my footsteps. I played my way across the meadow grass. Through my head went the buzz that lifted and encouraged—only a man headed for God's temple would move with steps as light as mine this morning.

I played, glancing up at the sky, so high above me, bright and cleansed by the morning.

Then, suddenly, I was overcome by a powerful roar, the whole earth seemed to shake with thunder, drowning out the buzzing in my head . . .

Whence was I going? In what direction was I headed? What did my eyes see as I walked? Where trod I now with my foot . . . ?

Who is silencing my comforting buzz? Who is thundering in my ears and drowning out my music? Who washes over my head, seizing my body? Who penetrates my mouth, closing off my throat? Who stops my breathing? Who is bursting my chest apart? Who is stifling my scream? Who is removing the world from me?

It is the spring.

THE SPRING

Thus, you must relinquish the world above under the sky. Thus, you sink down into me, weighed down by your own body. Into my depth falls silver and gold. Thus, you have come back to me, Piper Anders, bringing your spoil with you.

You thought that you would be allowed to bring your spoil to your god. You thought you would be able to rob me of the treasure that had been brought and pledged to me in honor of my deity. I have now reclaimed my property.

My depth is gilded once more. In my depth, the rays of my deity shine once again. As before, I carry my master's colors within my womb.

I was here long before your kind. In the beginning, my master and god opened me. My sun god was thirsty, and he let my veins flow. So, I rose up into the daylight and was revealed to the brightest light in the firmament. I loved my master's burning lips; together, his thirst and my flow fertilized the soil. Grasses and flowers grew, and all living things were created, nourished by us. We still perform our tasks in concert—his burning rays from the sky are cooled by the jets from my depths; and at our encounter, we beget life.

From me spring all the generations that have passed through this world. Of me were you born, Piper Anders! But now, you have come back. After all your life's shiftlessness, you are once more secure in my keeping. On light feet, you wandered into the room where you are to stay. Here is your abode. I have reclaimed you along with your booty, and you have brought it all back to me. You have repaid your debt.

At the vigil of your equals, you shall play your pipe and lead the dancers as the uncounted ring of years roll across the earth. Now, I call forth another wind player up onto the spelman's seat— Buckhorn!* You are to be found at several oak ages back in time, yet to me, you remain close always. Your time has come. Step forth and let us hear your music!

Piper Anders, listen now to him who was your predecessor as spelman in your family! He hails from the time when the winds were always balmy, when the grass stood tall and the thickets were dense, when my water mirrored the antlers of the watering stags, and when the nights of the brides were wondrously warm.

He is the last one to play at this spelman's vigil—the youngest and the oldest.

It is Buckhorn who plays in the night of the Sun's Holy Feast. It is in the golden age of the oak trees, when the god of procreation reigns alone.

---

* Cf. Swedish *Bockhorn*. The word for male goat in Old English was *bucca* (which now exists as the word *buck*, meaning any male herbivore) until a shift to he-goat/she-goat occurred in the late twelfth century. Nanny goat originated in the eighteenth century and billy goat in the nineteenth.—Tr.

Time IV

I, BUCKHORN:

He stands erected at the top of the hill right in our midst. He is freshly blood-stained and still drips like a sapping birch tree. The robe that covers his body gleams red in the light from our bonfires. In the gloom, he seems to grow before us and rises high under the mass of light-colored oak leaves.

This is He, whose name no one will speak.

Under the oaks, he rises to three men's height. His seed member is of one man's length, narrowing toward the head, and thickening around the fullness of the neck. His member has been painted red, like his body.

Here we are, men and women, gathered around our godhead on the hill.

The night is mild and without wind. Branch and leaf are at rest. The hawks and cocks, strung up among the oak branches, hang motionless like the leaves. Hook bill hangs by hook bill, spear beak by spear beak, and not one will ever catch again. There is hawk by hawk in the trees, yet not one will ever again swoop down to clutch with its talons. Blind eye next to blind eye stares out into the night, dead hawk next to dead hawk hangs, their talons slack, their necks drooping. Thickened blood pearls drip from the branches down onto the ground.

There, in the trees, hang the nine buck goats, completely flayed, glowing white against the green leaves. Below them, on the ground, stand the brimming blood kettles. Blood drips from the neck wounds. The grass under the oaks glistens red. Their curled horns have been left in place and adorn the white-flayed skulls of the beasts.

The sun is at its peak—this is the Brides' Feast, for which we have all gathered around our godhead on the hill. We are in danger. Our tribe is dwindling, and our might is weakening. We have come to him who can counsel us, that we may make amends to him in order that he may give new life to our people.

This is the sun's holy feast—the night is warm, our godhead burns red, and the wombs of the women await us.

But by the spring waits the maiden, our pledged sacrifice. Our tribe is in danger, and this maiden will we give Him for our salvation. Through her, he shall be appeased—she has been saved and readied for him. When we light our sun wheels here this night, we shall proffer her into the depth of his spring.

It is Tuah, she who was to have been mine at the Brides' Feast.

On this night of the holy Sun Feast we play—I, Buckhorn, and three others, each with his giga.* Here I am, and I shall play to please him, our god on the hill.

The horn I am blowing into comes from the first buck I ever felled.

I remember the hunt well. My father had fashioned a new arrow for me with a good, sharp tip. It was during the hottest season, and my father had taught me how to call the bucks. They were by now

---

* *Giga*: cf. *rababah*, *rebec*, precursor to the fiddle. Oblong or triangular body with two or three strings, producing a sharp tone.—Tr.

in full rut. I had observed their hoof marks in the wet grass at morning time, and I knew the spot they went to. I was in the grove before sunrise and lay down in the thicket to wait. Hidden by the leaves of beech and elm, I lay, my new arrow hooked on the string. To my lips, I held a fresh-cut elm leaf, and I blew the doe's call to the buck. I had practiced it for a long time, and now I could play the call on my leaf when the bucks were in their time of rutting.

As it grew light, he came forth. I lay downwind from him. I lay still as the earthbound stone and held back my breathing as I caught sight of him. The buck lifted his head way up high and sniffed. I saw his nose move, he was that near. He was old and had stout, splendid horns. I wanted him within closer reach of my bow, so I put the leaf to my lips once more and blew. At the sound, he raised his nose and sniffed again, and then he leapt toward the thicket where I lay waiting. He appeared somewhat dizzy as he moved. I took aim at his neck, where the blood runs thickest, and let my arrow fly.

The buck fell, kicking up sods of grass. The arrow had sunk deep within his flesh; its pink tip had done its work well. I wrested it out, put my mouth to the neck hole, and drank. The buck's blood ran sweet and warm down my throat. His force passed from him to me.

As I skinned my prey, I saved one of the horns. It formed a hook that curved closely around my hand. With the tip of my skinning knife, I bored a hole in the small end of the horn. I had tried my skill at playing and blowing on leaves. Now, I tried blowing in the hole of the goat horn. I brought forth many sounds. I bored a second hole for my thumb, which I removed and put back again, and I made yet other sounds. The braying of the doe had been easy to feign; but now, I could bellow like the bull and scream like the stallion as well.

I bored holes in the horn for two of my fingers. Then, I was satisfied. Now, I could caw like a crane, screech like a woodpecker, chirp like a finch, and coo like a dove. It became so I could echo any sound heard from the throat of a bird.

The circle of the year had not yet completed itself from the day when I felled the buck ere I was the foremost bird mimic amongst us, I, who until now had been able only to blow on leaves.

Tuah, from afar, had heard all the sounds I coaxed from the buck horn, and, one evening, she came over to me.

I was sitting on the turf outside our hut attempting to draw more sounds from the horn. Inside, my father lay asleep. I was alone. So, she came to listen at close quarters. I blew for her all the bird mimic sounds I knew—I was dove and raven, I was heron and hoopoe. I played, and she listened, laughing, while she moved ever closer to me on the heaped turf. She was yet slender as a lamb of limb and thigh.

I told her to name any animal, whichever she pleased, and I would let her hear its sound. Tuah named the animals, as many as she could think of, and I sounded it, each and every one, with my horn—and she clapped her hands together in wonder.

Tuah asked to borrow my horn. I let her handle it. She put it to her lips, but the sounds she made resembled more the spluttering of porridge in the pot, and we both laughed.

I wanted to play her own name for her. Tuah . . . like a small, puny bird I would hear among the leaves in the morning but had never seen in full. This bird sound was divided: *ooo-aaah!* Thus, I blew her name: *tuu-aaah! Tuuuu-aaaaah! Tuuuuuu-aaaaaa!*

Tuah sat quite still when she heard this. She asked me to blow it again, over and over, and I did as she asked. I believe she was glad to hear her name sound from my horn.

From then on, she had two names—one we all knew her by, and one that I played on my buck horn—one that was known to me alone.

One day, she said that she would give me a name in return, so that I, too, would have two—from this day on, she would call me Buckhorn.

I already had a name that everyone used. But from Tuah, I received a name to be known by. And by this name, everyone began to call me. My other name was slowly forgotten. Soon, I was called nothing but Buckhorn. I did not mind it.

At our next holy feast, I had my horn with me, and I was invited to join the giga players at the sacrifices and the dancing.

Evenings, I would meet Tuah by the watering troughs where she would lead her father's cattle in the grazing season. I played for her, mimicking new birds I had heard around the countryside. She sat quietly and listened. Her eyes shone clear as the water in the hollowed-out logs from which the beasts would drink, where it dripped from muzzle and hair. The goat skin fit closely around her loins and breasts, the skirt covering her tender kneecaps. Sometimes, she would sing to me in return, slowly and softly. There were no words—they were guarded by her lips. But what she sang was a song—one of these strange and wonderful songs that need no words.

The god Tjalve* had given Tuah very fleet feet at her birth. Every time when the maidens raced one another, she would fly across the fields like a feather in the wind, leaving all others behind. As she ran over the grass and stone, her hair like a floating bird's wing behind her, we young men all followed her with our eyes.

---

* Tjalve traveled in the service of the god Thor to Utgård, the realm of the giants. Utgårdaloke, the king of the giants, arranged several contests to amuse the company, and Tjalve offered to run a race against any man and was given a small boy, Hugi, for a competitor. Tjalve was soundly defeated and mortified until the following day, when King Utgårdaloke revealed that the little chap was none other than thought itself, which none can outrun.—Tr.

Out in the countryside, I would blow often that song that was her name:

"Too-aaa! Tooo-aaaa! Tooooo-aaaaa!"

If she was within hearing, she would answer by calling the name she knew me by:

"Buckhorn!"

Thus, we had our special calls for one another and could reach each other with our voices from afar.

Now, I had a name I could call when I roamed the country-side, and someone who listened. If you called a name repeatedly, its owner would at last come forth—even if he were dead and lifted onto the pyre, still, he would come at last, if you only kept calling long enough.

Since three winters, I had been without a woman in my hut. Dieyret, who had borne me a son, vanished one stormy night during the great snow winter, captured by our enemies or torn by wild animals, I never knew which. For a long time, I kept wandering all over the countryside in search of her tracks, but she remained lost. I missed Dieyret long after I had ceased looking for her. I missed her less since that evening when Tuah heard my horn and came and sat by me on the turf.

Dieyret's and my son was being raised by her parents, and I lived alone in our hut with my father, who was unsteady with age. That summer when I played at the holy feast of our godhead for the first time, I was forced to go out in search for my father in the fields one evening where he lay, unable to get up again. It happened several times more, and I would have to carry him home. By the time the cattle were being driven home from pasture, my father failed to get up from his bed one morning. I looked at him but asked no questions.

But after he had failed to rise for three mornings, he called me over to him and told me I could take the club to him when evening came.

I did as I had been told. I gathered food and drink and called our friends to my father—there were yet a few who could walk upright, and they walked on limping legs and looked around them with dim eyes. When evening fell, I took the ash club in my hand and my father on my back and walked out into the meadow, accompanied by my father's friends.

I had to shorten my stride so as to allow the old ones to keep up on their limping legs. My father knew of a fair, flat spot. That is where he instructed me to go, and that is where we stopped. We ate sweet bread and goat cheese and drank mead made from the autumn crop of barley. We became somewhat merry, and all of us talked much. My father spoke long about his youth, of women who had been in his possession and use, of a man's duty to know when his time had come, and of the shame of prolonging his days on the sickbed, so humiliating to him. Last, he spoke of the club blow, which it was a man's last act of honor to request.

Time and again, we drank to the memories. We drank to Him, whose real name no one mentioned. We did not fail to honor any memory that evening in the meadow.

Dusk began to fall, and my father declared that the time had come. He grasped the hands of his friends, one after the other. Last, he clasped mine—his last wish in life was that his son should acquit himself honorably before all his friends and strike a good blow.

He then lay down on the ground and beckoned to me with his head. He was ready. He was waiting. He had asked of me a strong man's deed. Slowly, I raised the club, calling on all my strength. I believe that my father, had he been able, would have judged the blow a good one. His skull was split in two, the blood welled from his nose and mouth, and he uttered no sound. His friends acknowledged that I had swiftly and faultlessly given him the club. I was highly praised.

I built a pyre of resinous fir wood and placed my father on it. A strong wind had been blowing all day, but as I lit the fire, it quieted, and the smoke rose straight up to the god in the sky. Our friends stayed and watched with me by the fire that was taking my father away from this earth.

Gullfåle, my father's white stallion that had been pledged to Him, stood dripping with sweat in his stall the next morning. I wiped the beast off with a handful of straw and was at ease—He had used my father's gift and been out riding his horse last night. From that, I could tell that my father had been well received.

Thus, I was left alone in my hut, waiting for Tuah to come to me.

Our chieftain had decreed many times that no young man should be without a woman. We were in need of new life. For the last few years, we had counted fewer born ones than burned ones. At the feast of the child-bearers at the last spring equinox, we counted only ten young women with new-sprung breasts. At earlier feasts of the child-bearers, we would rejoice over as many as thirty women giving suck for the first time. These signs of infertility spread great anxiety among us. We feared our numbers would thin out to the point where our enemies would feel bold enough to creep nearer to our fields.

Tuah had lost some of her kid slenderness. She had grown— her thighs were rounded, and her breasts had filled out. Her womb was strong enough to give birth. Tuah was one of the maidens who would be ready for a man at the coming feast of the brides. She was the one that the eyes of the young men most gladly followed.

She was a maiden of few words, and shy; yet, when she sang to me at the watering troughs at night, I could read the signs beneath her eyelids—she wanted to come to me. I began to believe that something would be consummated between us next time we celebrated our Sun Feast.

But when spring came and the first green growth shone throughout our fields, death fell over our cattle.

The first one was Silvermanke, our chieftain's sacred ox. Silvermanke dropped one evening at the watering troughs. He gave forth a great bellow and lay there, his legs straight out and his tongue hanging out of his mouth. He lay as though felled by a club blow between his horns—he was dead. Sudden death had struck down an animal that was dedicated to Him, and we all saw this as an ill omen.

Anxious over our cattle, we drove our beasts out to pasture earlier than what used to be our wont. Yet, in the fields, our beasts found themselves entirely at the mercy of the sickness. Every evening, an ox or a cow would be missing at the watering troughs. The missing ones would be found dead in the pasturage, their limbs and tongues outstretched.

We lit spark fires and drove the animals over them; but the disease came to the horses also. Gullfåle, who was dedicated to Him, was tethered each night in the grassy grove near my hut. One morning as I stepped out under the open sky, I could see the stallion nowhere. But I saw a raven sitting on his tether post, and I well could guess the rest. Sure enough—my stallion lay dead in a hollow, his yellow teeth bared.

Horses, oxen, cows, and calves fell in droves in the grazing season. We were digging day and night to bury the carcasses. Heat began to set in, and there was a foul stench from the deceased carrion, surrounded by dense, buzzing swarms of flies. We lit fires on the hills until the smoke settled over all our fields. We extinguished the last spark from the old, noxious fire in our mines. We lit spark fires inside all our huts. We meant to leave nothing untried.

Still, our cattle kept dying on us, and we lay the beasts in the ground with great sadness.

From all the dead stallions and bulls, we cut and saved the pizzles to dry them and keep for the feast of the brides, when they would be boiled and eaten by the men—such food would make men giddy with breeding power and give them great bridegroom lust.

The evil death took away our goats and sheep as well. During the day, the fly swarms grew ever more numerous and thick. Over our carrion, the blue flies would drone their buzzing songs. They sounded vicious and threatening to our ears and presaged danger.

Day and night, our fires burned, but they could not consume the ravager.

We wanted to spare no effort at placating him. We buried bunches of flax and onion in the earth. From our young beasts, we selected two beautiful heifers, dug a deep grave, and placed them within it without killing them. We reckoned that the cattle that were left to us would be spared from now on. The heifers mooed and bellowed quite anxiously as we covered them with dirt in their grave.

Every evening we counted our remaining cattle by the watering logs. At each sundown, our women would be milking ever fewer udders of cow and goat. With ever slower steps, they carried home ever lighter growing milk pails. Our cattle, our might, our riches turned to rot and carrion before our eyes. From the meat and milk and cheese that were our food, the flies would strike up their death buzz; from the wool and hair and skin in our clothes, the winged beasts would sing their farewell. And once they finished buzzing over the last animal carcass in the grass, the turn would come to all of us. We would indeed know hunger as never before. Over our bodies, bigger birds with larger wings would be hovering. Were we to lose our beasts, it would mean our certain death.

In two months' time, one-third of our cattle died.

Ever fewer of our women gave birth. The feast of the child-bearers was held with only five women giving suck. To our anxiety over cattle dying in greater and greater number, we now added worry over the infertility of our women.

By the time we reached the Sun Feast, fear had us thoroughly in its grip. Our women would set to wailing over the milk pails; our men went about with stiff faces with no expression. We invoked our godhead and asked:

"To what aim grows the blade of grass, if not to be bitten off by the horse's teeth, ripped off by the ox's tongue? Why is the rich grass covering our valleys and slopes in its plenty if not to feed our beasts so they can give us their meat and hides, wool and cheese, milk and cream? Is the sun to travel its course and shine over wasted land, covered by carrion and carcasses?"

He must be appeased, he who reigned over sun and weather, he who had power over all beasts, he who ruled over all life in field, forest, and meadow.

Our counsel met and deliberated over the ultimate sacrifice.

We thought we had neglected nothing. Yet, the ultimate sacrifice to Him was yet to be made. Many years had passed since it had last been made. Now, he was requiring it of us. Now, we would not be let off. We would make the sacrifice—a young woman yet untouched, the most treasured, the dearest one of all our maidens.

Who was she, the most prized of all our maidens? Who was she, the most precious that our tribe could give? Who was the one most desired by the men? Who gave the greatest gladness to the young men's eyes? We all knew her name—it hardly needed saying. I would never have spoken it at the counsel had they whipped me with a hundred bull pizzles, yet it changed nothing—no one could deny that the maiden's name was the name I carried within my horn and which I would sound all through the fields and meadows: Tuah.

In the evening of the day the counsel was held, she was led from her parents' hut to the shrine of the godhead near our settlement. She who ran on her legs so swiftly, swifter than any of our other young maidens, now walked so quietly between the chieftain's two guards. Her light-colored hair no longer floated behind her like a bird at large, but hung heavily down her back like a broken wing. Our godi* had donned his festival robes and walked ahead of her. Her father and mother followed and completed the procession to the god shrine.

Tuah no longer belonged to us. Now, she was his consecrated maiden. Henceforth, she would be like one of his trees, like one of his hills, she was like his waters and his streams. She was no longer of our kind; we were but to keep her in readiness for the feast.

Three days and three nights were left until the night of the Sun Feast, on which we would deliver her. Woe unto us, then, if she was no longer untouched! Woe unto us if anything were to happen to her before that day!

Pairs of men took turns guarding the shrine where Tuah was kept. There, people came to worship her and fall on their knees before her, offering her gifts as if she were one of his holy trees or waters. Our tastiest food was carried to her. Sweet bread and honey was prepared, doves and thrushes were cooked, the women brought her trinkets, gold and silver.

But I, Buckhorn, did not sleep on my bed in my hut. I roamed around the house where Tuah was. I walked in wide circles; I did

---

* Sacrificial priest; priest and chieftain in pre-Christian Scandinavian culture.—Au.

not come near on account of the guards. I carried my horn with me, but I did not put it to my lips, I never played it. When it grew light, I returned to my hut again.

There, I lay on my bed all day and thought of him, our god on the hill. We were all in his power. No one could escape that power. He was in the sky above our heads. He was in the ground beneath the soles of our feet. He was in the air that flowed into our mouths. He ruled over the ray that guided our eyes and gave us light. His fires rolled across the sky. He was in the grass, the leaves, the trunks and the logs, in brooks and springs. He was within us and outside. No one could detach himself from him. He was the all powerful, the unreachable.

And unreachable as the rays of the sun was all that belonged to him. Tuah, whose coming to my hut I had been waiting for, now that she had grown and become ready for a man, she had now become his property.

Next evening, I went out again to walk my circles around the godhead shrine.

Then, I caught sight of two toads sitting by the threshold of my hut. I noticed that the toads were of a quite formidable size. Yet, I walked on without paying them any attention. I would not be cautioned by the creatures with the evil portents.

Scarce had I walked one circle around the house where Tuah was kept before a powerful flash of lightning streaked across the sky. It flashed right over my head, quicker than my eye could blink. At first, I stood still, crouched and trembling. Then, I ran. I ran as I had never run before, back to my hut—He would come after me as soon as I would dare get near his shrine. He was striking at me with his fire

He was guarding her.

Next morning, the toads still sat there and waited outside my doorstep, big and fat like piglets. They sat motionless, opening their poisonous mouths to me. Yet, now, I had been forewarned. I knew the toads to be his guardian beasts. They were watching me. They had followed me during my wanderings last night, though I had not noticed them in the darkness. Were I to take one step toward the spot where Tuah was, the toads would come after me.

That day, I did not once step across my threshold. I did not walk past his animals. I stayed within my hut.

I trembled before him whose rightful name no one spoke. I, Buckhorn, became like the puniest leaf, quivering in the tree at its branch hold. No more did I walk my rings around the house that held his property.

Yet one day and one night remained before the Brides' Feast on the hill, when she would be proffered.

Below the hill ran the spring out of the black soil. To us, she was the mother who gave to all of us her fresh, white suck. Her dugs were never empty when we lay down over her, reaching our thirsty lips toward her. The spring was a mother with inexhaustible breasts which we, her children, could suck at our will. When all other waters had run dry and were gone, our spring would still be left to us. Her clear jets would still flow, refreshing us when the woes of thirst set in. The spring was our gentle mother.

But her depth was misty as a wet autumn night. Down there dwelt darkness in its chamber, and into this chamber, He would welcome her. We would send her down there. When the night of the Sun Feast reached its darkest moment, then, she would be proffered.

I had been forewarned, and I now shrank in terror at the thought of what I had dared for two nights. The third and last night, I stayed at home in my hut.

That was when Tuah came to me.

It was while I lay sleeping. I did not hear her as she walked through the door. I heard no footsteps across the floor. Yet, my hands felt her in my bed. Here, right with me, she was. She pressed her loins against mine. Fiercely, I reached for her, my hands clasping around her back as I held her close to me. Like the willowy branch, her body fit itself to mine. I felt entirely contented—she was with me, and I knew no fear.

And Tuah breathed warmth into my ear with her words: "Buckhorn! Help me, Tuah! Take me away from Him! I do not want to go down there, into the water, where darkness lives. I want to stay up here under the sun. I want to run like I used to beneath the great heavenly light! I want to hear your horn speak my name until it resounds among bushes and trees! I want to come to your hut, prepare your food, and lie near you on your bed! I am full grown and ready for you. I can be one of the brides at the feast! I do not want to be lowered down to him! I want to stay up here! I wish to stay under the sun, the moon, and the bright stars! You, Buckhorn! Help me, Tuah! Take me away from him!"

I clasped her tightly as her words flowed into my ear. I answered Tuah and gave her my promise.

But, in a moment, she had slipped away from me. I found myself suddenly alone in my bed, fumbling around with my hands, grasping for my own body.

I was awake and could see no trace of Tuah in the hut.

I became frightened and sprang up. It was light; day was dawning. I opened the door. Outside sat his toads, waiting, gaping, their swollen bellies heaving. A slow breeze blew among the heavy, dewy leaves of the thickets. I could see nothing of Tuah, I could hear nothing, no matter how hard I listened. It was not her whole body that had passed through my door—she had walked neither in nor out.

The whole being that was Tuah remained in his chamber, in her place of keeping. It was only her shade that had come to me—it was her wraith that had been lying there with me last night. Her wraith had sought me to bring me her message—her wish. As I had been unable to get near Tuah on account of the beasts that guarded her, her wraith had visited my hut.

It was not the first time a woman's shade had come to me at night. I remembered. I returned to my bed and found what I expected—my seed had been spilled.

Suddenly, I stood quite still, my breath growing heavy. It had happened last night on my bed, while the beasts sat guarding outside. She had come and driven away my fear, and it had happened—I had desecrated her who belonged to Him. Here, on my bed, I had broken the seal of his holy maiden.

Now, he would wreak his vengeance upon me!

There lay the spilled seed that was to have been saved for the Brides' Feast. Yet, the sign was that it had been given to her—something had now been consecrated between Tuah and me. I had given her my word, and this consecration of loin to loin was beyond revoking.

Henceforth, Tuah and I could no longer be parted.

I, Buckhorn, am now playing on this night of the Brides' Feast, voices of horn and giga blending. Our tribe has gathered around our god on the hill.

The peace of the sacred feast has been declared. The men's hands are loose and free of all fighting weapons, contenting themselves with the skinning knives only, with which they would cut away the meat from the bones of the slaughtered animals. There they hang from the oak trees now, his bucks, bathed in their own coursing blood, dripping down on us from their necks. There hang his sacred birds—hawks gazing down on us from the trees, their eyes without light. On the neck-wrung cocks, the red, spiny combs gleam. In a ring under the trees stand the meat kettles, filled to the brim with our sacrificial fare. Large wicker baskets hold what will be turned into man's drink—hen's eggs, white and brown, large and small. And, around the place of our gathering, stand the far-sheltering oaks, dark and still. High above our heads, they stretch their gnarly limbs that seem, in the dark, like snakes entwined in their nest.

The Brides' Feast has begun. The barren women begin offering their prayers to Him. Their heads are covered. They all have men, but none of these women has borne a child to her man. Now, the whole flock of them walks to the top of the hill, each kneeling and embracing his member with both arms. All of us are silent for as long as the barren ones remain in their position of worship, their arms around him:

"Help us, our god! Make our wombs fruitful! Our tribe is in danger—grant us life, o, our god on the hill!"

The summer bride is the spring child-bearer. The sun will run through nine signs, the moon rise up new nine times. Then, we will gather for the Child-Bearers' Feast. Our god, open new breasts with healthy suck! We are in danger! Give life to our tribe!

The hawks among the curling oak branches look down with blind, staring eyes on the barren women as they clasp his red member.

The women slowly rise from their kneeling and slowly walk back to us. On the light-colored belts around their waists, red blotches are showing. He gives off his wetness like the birch-tree with its sappy bark in spring. This is a lucky omen.

In the sky, the sun has passed its highest point. The short night is here, when his tribute shall be given. Tonight, we will hold our flaming wheels over the hill, so that he will bless the ground and give us growth and harvest. To us, the mighty one on the hill seems to swell and grow larger in the dark that surrounds us.

Giga and buck horn strike up their playing. We sound the chirping of the finch, the cry of the woodpecker, the cooing call of the dove. We play the stallion's scream, the bull's bellow, the buck's bleating at the peak of his rut. We play the sounds that come out of furry throats, hairy and feathered necks, out of bodies that fly on the wing and run on the hoof, that rip with their claws and tear with their teeth. We play all the sounds you hear in woods and fields, glades and meadows.

We evoke our god with giga and horn. We urge him, whose name must not be spoken:

"Our tribe is in danger!"

I am not lacking for breath tonight as I blow into my horn. I blow out my air from a taut chest, out of a full lung chamber. Yet, it is not out of my own breast that I am blowing; my horn plays out of the bosom of the ground, the beasts, the waters, the trees, and all the grasses.

It is the night of gifts and sacrificial fare on our hill. The beasts give their flesh. From the bucks, every limb is cut away, the skinning knives scraping the bones clean. Our men eat the pizzles that have been saved and boiled—the flesh that makes a man fit for breeding. Our hens give their eggs for the drink that will strengthen the bridegrooms. The eggs are poured from the baskets, then crushed and stirred. The bridegrooms' drink of might is yellow as gold, white as silver. It runs heavy and viscous into the ladles. Like golden rivulets, the sacrificial drinks flow in our vessels. Kettles and dippers are emptied. We are making ready for the mating hour.

Our food is hot; our women are rank and eager. We play for him out of overflowing bosoms. He rules over the green spring, the yellow summer, over the red autumn and the blue winter. His is the fresh herb, the yellow wheat ear. His is the red leaf and the blue ice. And his is the water in the spring who gives suck to all life in forest and field.

Men and women dance their circles around the red one on the hill. He is raised up tonight on his sacred shrine. He rises among the green oaks like a thick tree with its branches lopped off. Around him, we dance on this night of the Sun Feast.

Our night is warm, our god glows red, and our women's wombs await us.

But, around the spring, a round spot lay secluded from the people. None of us would tread on it with our foot. Within that circle, our pledged sacrifice stood waiting, the one who would be offered when the night was at its darkest. Around her stood the men who were set to watch and guard her. The guards were our strongest men. Each had placed his hands over his member, swearing by this, his chief limb and body part, to protect His property. Sooner would they give their lives than let anyone touch the promised sacrifice.

By the spring, Tuah waited.

She was standing in the midst of the circle, dressed in the same color he wore—she was clad in the red robe. Her hair was bound over her back with red ribbons, no longer free to float like bird's wings. From where I sat on the hill, I could see her face, white as the gnawed and weather-bleached bones we found in the woods.

Close by her, I saw the black face of a man. At Tuah's side stood our godi with his festival robes on. He had prepared himself and smeared his face with the sacred mud from the bottom of the spring. The face of our godi was colored black like its depth. Still and motionless he stood, waiting by our pledged sacrifice. Just as still, without moving body or limb, hand or foot, stood the guards around them.

Two faces were visible by the spring—a man's and a woman's, one black, the other white.

Last night, I had touched the sacred maiden, and I had been awaiting His revenge. Yet, I sat here still, free to follow my own counsel, my body unharmed. Was I unreachable to him? I had wondered. I had made a decision—I would attempt to thwart him.

Within the circle by the spring, Tuah waited, pledged to him. But I was the one she was waiting for.

I had hidden it well. Well before the beginning of our feast, I had concealed it within the lush nut tree, only a few steps from the spring. There it lay, safely hidden, waiting for my hands and the right moment. I had selected it carefully and practiced with it. The stone was of the right size and weight for me to throw.

Through her wraith, Tuah came to my bed last night. Her loins, soft and pliant as the willow branch, had nestled close to mine. She was good to me, as a woman can be. I had been soothed and released from all my fear. She had already received my seed—it happened the night before our feast on the hill.

She had asked me to take her away from him, and I had given her my word. I would keep my promise.

The thick oaken leaf walls began blackening around us. He who stood on the hill was beginning to dim before our eyes. Night had reached its darkest moment. Now, the sun wheels would be lit to give us light while we made our promised sacrifice.

He must be placated.

We had ceased playing. Men and women gathered around the spring, but the inner circle was still kept free by the guards. I sat down under the largest oak, near my blooming nut tree, my hiding place, within close reach.

Everyone became quiet. A mild breeze blew among the oak leaves. The neck-wrung hawks and cocks swayed from their branches. Our godi turned his face, blackened by the spring's muck, toward him on the hill. Nine times, he spoke the urgent incantation of atonement. The sign had been given.

The ones who were to light our fires stepped inside the inner circle, the sun wheels in their hands. They bored and struck, while all of us waited in silence for the fire. I made haste, knowing the light would come soon. I retrieved the stone from beneath the tree and hid it under my hands, between my crossed knees. Then I sat motionless like the trunk of an oak once more.

The fire came quickly, seizing the dry straw. The wheels caught flame and threw their light all around and over all of us. The men who had lit them hurried to drop the flames out of their hands, and the sun's burning wheels rolled across the ground. The sparks from the fire flew over our heads, up toward the treetops like hovering butterflies. I followed them with my eyes. One spark flew into a hollow where birds were building their nest. Above me, I saw the gnarly oak branches wind into a snarl of thick, bloated snakes.

One by one, the wheels were lit, rolled around, and shone on our godhead on the hill. His member was aflame in the firelight.

Our godi held the chalice out to Tuah. I could not see whether her lips touched it, if she drank or not. Her limbs were bound, her mouth was shut and mute. The sparks from the sun wheels flitted about her light-colored hair. The red butterflies of the Sun Feast swarmed around her head in the night. I did not see her move at all.

But our godi touched her forehead, painted her with the sacred mud. Now, Tuah already wore the marks of the depth on her face.

I crouched near the root of the large oak. Concealed under my hands, between my knees, lay the stone, the one that was of the right weight to be thrown. I felt my tendons tighten—I was ready to spring. I would defy Him.

Then, I heard a sound, like the chirping of a young bird. It seemed to me that it came from above my head, from the oak. I glanced up at the trunk, where the birds had built their nests in the hollows. The leaves rustled faintly. It might be a bird flying in or out of its hollow; I could not see it. But I saw something else in the oak above me:

I saw the snakes.

Just then, our godi gave the sign to the guards. Two tall men stepped forth, grasped her arms, lifted her between them, and carried her to the spring. It would take no more than a few steps.

I had made as if to leap. Yet I sat where I sat, crouching under the oak. The snakes up there had begun to move at the same time as I.

My eyes had been fooling me earlier tonight. It was not the oak branches that had resembled snakes; it was the snakes up there in the tree that had appeared to me as gnarly oak branches. I had misread what I saw among the leaves in the dark. Now, I knew what had frightened the little bird that flew among the leaves—a snake lay curled, waiting, in the net of branches over my head. It would lie still within the oak for as long as I sat here quietly. When I moved as if to leap, the snake bundle would move slowly forward . . .

It was his creature. He was protecting his property. He was watching me still.

I remained seated under the oak, without moving, my face turned upward. My hands which were holding the stone began to tremble. He still had me in his power.

They stood still and held her over the opening. A large fire wheel rolled by, and in its glow, I saw her between the men. Her bare feet were bound together. When they reached the water, she lifted them and sought to hold them above it. She bent her knees, held her feet up, and shrank away from the water. Her bound hands moved, seeking purchase, fumbling for the men's shoulders.

I clenched my jaws and, once more, readied myself to spring. But as I looked up again into the oak, I saw the nest of snakes move, creep forward, slowly creeping right above my body. I saw the heads of the snakes, saw their fangs jut out, angry and red.

Before I would have had time to move hand or foot, the cursed snakes would have wreathed down across my back. I remained motionless, crouching. My very body had become a stone, too heavy to lift.

Once more, silence reigned all around, among all men and women. The sun wheels alone sputtered and hissed out their sparks. They were burned out, consumed, had sunk down into ashes and were extinguished, while new ones were lit in place of the ones that had burned down.

I could hear a splashing sound in the water. It sounded as if something weighty had been dropped down into it, a stone or a log. Yet, of a sudden, there was life and movement within the spring—something was thrashing and clamoring violently.

There came a scream from the spring.

At that sound, the two men bent over the spring once more. The screaming ceased. The men straightened up again, and all was silent.

It was not a log. There was one scream, a short one. Then, the spring water was quiet once more.

I lay prostrate at the foot of the oak. My body shook, my limbs felt as though they were broken. Weakly, my hands fumbled with the stone, that stone that would have been just heavy enough for me to throw. I put my hands to my mouth and bit into them, drawing blood from my fingers in my rage, in my powerlessness. I had not been able to defy Him.

It stayed quiet now, the snake bundle in the tree. I lay at the foot of the oak, biting my useless hands into shreds.

No more sounds were heard from the spring. All the people waited. Our godi waited. The guards by the opening waited, the fire starters rolled no more wheels—everyone was waiting.

Then, finally, our godi reached up into the sky with his hands— the waiting was over. At that, the men bent down over the opening of the spring. There were more sounds to be heard from the water— calm, soft, clucking sounds, and there were no more screams. They lifted, but no limbs moved, no knees were bending, no feet were raised in avoidance of the spring.

They brought her up, and she was limp, quite still, easy to handle. Her head fell to one side and rested on one shoulder.

They carried her over to where I sat. They hung her up into the largest one of the oaks. At the trunk of the oak, I still sat, I, Buckhorn.

Then, our godi raised up his hands and heralded it—in a high, piercing voice, he gave our tribe the joyful tidings:

He had received her at once. The wait had been very brief. This meant that our gift had been wanted. It meant that he was placated. It meant that we would all be spared.

Shrieks of great joy then burst forth from the throats of men and women:

"Our night has borne fruit! Our godhead is appeased! We are saved!"

The night of the Sun Feast has passed its darkest moment. It is growing light around him who stands on the hill.

The Brides' Feast has reached its hour of completion.

Newly lit sun wheels roll over the grass. Dancers are beginning to form rings. We begin to hear the songs—the songs of breeding, the songs of the bridal beds, the songs in praise of his service, the songs about the red one up there:

"We shall ready our beds
'Neath the sheltering oaks
Before His eyes,
Our worship complete.
We shall show Him, the red one,
Remind and prove to Him
What we ask of Him, and He will know.
See it, He will,
And grant it, He will.
Our tribe is in danger!
Grant us life, our god!

"To serve the almighty, we gather,
Men and women all,
Seeking each other,
Embracing each other,
Our lives to secure.
As near to each other as shapes will allow,
Mingling till two are as one.

"Man, find woman's breast!
Woman, find man's limb and loins!
Men, give forth your power!
Women, receive men's power!
Thus, we breed, our lives to prolong;
To stretch through times eternal!

"Tonight is the feast of the brides.
Nine months hence, we celebrate
The Child-Bearers' Feast
When new breasts are opened
And old ones anew give suck.
You, up there on your hill,
You see us now,
Stretched out before your eyes,
By your sacred shrine.
In this night of the Sun Feast shall we serve you,
And, in return, you shall be appeased
And bless us with your gifts:
Our tribe is in danger!
Give life to us, our god!

"Bright and warm is our night.
Our god is appeased and mild,
And the wombs of the women await us."

Yet, by the large oak, I, Buckhorn, still sat. I was alone. In my hand rested my horn, taken from my first felled buck. I did not play it.

All around me, the feasting was held in his honor. All around me, our godhead was invoked to bless our mating. Yet, I sat alone by the trunk of the oak.

They were calling:

"Buckhorn! Are you seated there still? Why do you remain alone? Find yourself a woman! Where have you hidden her? Where is your woman, Buckhorn?"

At their calling, I raised my head somewhat. I was again reminded of where I had my woman.

She was strung up in the large oak. Among the golden cock's combs and the hooked beaks of the hawks, I could see her hanging. I remained where I sat.

Again, above me, I could hear the sound from the puny little bird that I might at times see among the multitude of leaves, yet had never seen in its entirety. There, in one of the hollows of the trunk, it was readying its nest. As I heard it anew, I remembered something else that was like the sound of that bird—something I used to play on my buck horn once. It was a name. It was divided into two sounds, sounds that came right back to me—I might be able to blow that name again, should I wish to.

She who owned it was up there in the oak, one full-grown man's height from me. She hung there like a bright fruit from the hold of the tree branch. Her head had fallen to one side and was resting on her shoulder. From the hawks and cocks on the branches surrounding her, red, viscous drips were falling. From her, glistening, white droplets fell—the clear water of the spring.

I put the horn to my lips and blew:

"Tuu-aah! Tuuuu-aaaah! Tuuuuuu-aaaaaah!"

I struck up so that my playing resounded all around the hill, and I kept my face upturned and looked at her. Her eyes were closed, but her mouth was open. White droplets trickled from her mouth and fell to the ground beneath her.

There, in the tree, hangs your woman, Buckhorn.

And I played for her. I blew into my horn:

"Tuuuuuu-aaaaaah!"

You could call them back by their names, could you not? They could be called back; they could come to life again. If only one called their names, for a long time. If only one kept calling long enough.

I blew into my horn for a long time.

The sun was beginning to shine over the hill, and I was blowing still. I sat by the oak trunk with the horn from my first buck, and I was alone. I blew long enough.

Yet, there was no answer. Her eyes remained closed; her mouth was agape; the droplets fell from her clothes; ever more slowly they fell, yet they kept on falling. The spring was still there within her. Her head had sunk and lay, unmoving, on the bed of one shoulder.

She did not answer the call of my horn. She did not come back, however persistently I called her name. Where was your woman, Buckhorn?

He had taken her.

It had grown light and it was almost daylight. I began to look around me. I looked up at the oak. The snarl of snakes had retreated. Now, all I saw up there were leaves, branches, and a small, puny bird jumping around from twig to twig. I saw no snake lying there, curled, no scales gleamed. The net of branches was free of crawling creatures. All I could see was a small wretch, jumping and singing. The day had dawned. His creatures had vanished.

He no longer watched me.

I was free. All my stolen powers were restored to my body. Now, I was strong enough to take that leap that I had been crouching in readiness for.

I flung my horn to the side and, instead, seized the stone that still lay between my knees. Now, I could throw it! Now, I could defy him!

I ran.

Sun wheels that were dying out lay right in my path. Smoldering fire crunched under my feet. I did not look where I was stepping. I stumbled over roots; I fell, fell, but quickly stood up again. I ran, raising the stone high over my head.

Then, someone called out a warning:

"Buckhorn! He is running! Look out for Buckhorn with the stone!"

I kept on running; I fell, stood up again; I did not stop.

They kept calling:

"Over here! Over here! Look where Buckhorn is running!"

I was almost there when a ring of men began to close in on me. Arms and legs reached for me, arms that sought to grasp, legs that sought to fell. I lifted my feet as before, but they now ran in place. I was pushed, kicked, trampled, and I stood where I was.

I screamed—screamed out of my full lung chamber:

"Give way! Give way for me, Buckhorn! To Him!"

From all side came the shouts:

"It has seized him, the spirit of madness! Over here! He is possessed by the spirit of madness. Bring the skinning knife here!"

But, the stone I was to throw? Where was my stone? Where had I my arms to throw it with?

"The skinning knife! The skinning knife! Stick him! Stick!"

Pain! Pain cuts through me.

"Stick! Stick! Stick!"

More pain! Pain! Pain!

I had defied him whose name no one must speak. Now, the ground rose up against me. Everything around was rising up against me, and everything evil was cutting through me.

I, Buckhorn, fell down before him on the hill.

THE SPRING

Yes, this is how you returned to me, Buckhorn, the oldest and the youngest of the spelmen. This is how it came to pass that the maiden was given to me, pure and untouched. It was she and none other that gave me my full power; this power shall I use for the healing and succor of women for as long as my water still flows here. This power is mine during the shortest night. It shall remain in my possession for as long as earth protects and shields my veins in its depth, and for as long as I have my origin right here at the foot of the hill.

For this reason am I called the brides' spring.

We at the Watch

Who are we, the men playing tonight on the hill under the oaks? Lira and fiddle sing, pipe and buck horn blow. It is Midsummer night; it is St. John's night; it is the night of the Sun Feast. It is the night without age.

The dancing is held around the maypole, around the tree, around the fire, around the godhead with the blood-smeared member. Here is the ring through the years that no one counts.

We have gathered here, we, the four spelmen of the same family. We are the ones who are playing. Here, we strike up lira and fiddle, buck horn and pipe, here, we strike up a ring dance that runs through all times.

We have returned to our gentle mother, who guards and keeps her own, who leaves no one to be lost in this world, who gathers all her children back into her arms. The world gave us its anguish and its torment. Our mother gives us neither anguish nor torment. Mercifully, she holds us to her soft bosom. She does not chide, she does not take us to task, she does not judge, she does not grieve. We are all equally dear to her; we are all equally safe in her keeping. She is our beneficent spring.

The generations pass through the world, and the gods are exchanged—yet, here, we remain. The oaks flourish in their youth, rot in their old age; yet, we remain as we were, as we are. The grass grows and wilts; the spring flows and runs dry according to the passing of time, yet we are eternal. Here, the same grasses keep whispering, the same water keeps purling, and the same skies will forever travel over us here.

Sound, strings and horns! Whirl your rings, ye dances! Here, we keep our vigil. Here, we keep our vigil all through a night without age.

We play the tunes that will never be new but will sound forever. Blossoms will open, buds will spring forth, the sun will shine, the rain will fall. We are the ones you hear playing. The wind blows where it will, the leaf rustles, and the wet hand of the morning dew touches leaf and blade . . . We are the ones you hear playing.

We are what will never be changed, who fear nothing and who long for nothing, who anticipate nothing, who desire nothing. We are those who know no anguish.

We are of the congregation of peace, and we play in the chamber of the unreachable.

Throughout the world, the ring of generations still dances with joy and sorrow, with pleasure and despair, with torment and lust. Our dancing circle spans what is beyond anxiety, beyond consolation. We play our strings in a chamber that lies west of sadness, east of happiness.

We know neither the past nor the future. We are motionlessness. We are immovable and unchanging, and we keep our vigil here by our mother—the spring that runs up here out of the earth's nether regions, whose veins no one has yet seen.

We are the many who keep our vigil here tonight. We are the generation of the countless. We are the rested ones.

We were of the world. We were lost. We have returned. This is our home. This is death.

Pipes, flutes, strings, resound! You, our motionless dance, ring around! The night of our vigil is long.

One day, you will all keep vigil with us, beyond sorrow, beyond happiness.